I0626231

T.A. Maxwell

Broken Like Vinyl

Broken Like Vinyl

Copyright © 2013 by T.A. Maxwell

Printed in the United States of America
First Printing, 2013
ISBN 0-9890182-6-1

Published by Zen Dog Publishing, U.S.A.

ta.maxwell@live.com
www.amazon.com/author/tamaxwell

For those battling with heartbreak and depression

.

Broken Like Vinyl

Love is a motherfucker.

RYAN

"So, do you know why you're here Ryan?" The man in the big brown leather chair says to me, the doctor, the shrink, the man who is supposed to fix me, or whatever. As I contemplate his question, he stares at me. I make eye contact with him, his hair is short and combed with that generic part that most professionals have. Think slimy politician. I break eye contact and move my eyes downward, judging his outfit now. He is wearing the typical costume of a professional, a solid light blue dress shirt with the sleeves rolled up to mid-forearm, a yellow paisley tie, khaki slacks, and brown shoes. His shoes are those slip-on ones with those stupid little tassels on them. I hate them, I hate him, I hate his hair and I really hate his outfit, but I must say I do love his socks. They are black and white and in a 3D checkerboard print. They don't match the rest of his outfit but they are pretty sweet regardless. I catch myself staring at them, zoning out, so I go back to the staring contest.

"What?" I say, even though I knew the question he had asked but I didn't have an answer yet so I was trying to stall.

"Do you know why you're here?" All I can think about is his stupid haircut as I stare at it trying to stall some more.

"I think I have a pretty good idea." I finally say as I stretch my arms into the air and then back behind me. I am sitting in a smaller, less expensive leather chair right across from him. A black boxy IKEA looking coffee table separates us, which doesn't match the chairs we are sitting in. It's actually pretty fucking tacky and all I can think about is how bad the Feng Shui is in this room.

"And what is that?"

He breaks my thought with his question and I start to stare at his ugly yellow paisley tie. I suddenly realize that while I have been judging his outfit he must be judging mine. I showed up to this appointment, which was not my doing by the way but my brothers, in my typical attire, black sweatpants and a Chive t-shirt. Today's shirt, my 3D Bill fucking Murray shirt, is my favorite. On my feet, classic Vans, black, with black no show socks. I look awesome and there is not a drop of sarcasm in that statement, I look like a fucking badass.

"Ryan, why do you think you're here?"

I snap out of it again, literally shaking away the cobwebs that have formed in my head. "Um, because my brother thinks I'm crazy."

"And do you agree with your brother?"

"Do I look crazy?" My voice is slightly raised.

He looks at my right forearm, which has a large bandage on it and I suddenly regret my response. "That's not what I asked. I want to know if you agree with his diagnosis." I stare at those tassels on his shoes. God, I hate those damn things. "Ryan, please, I need a little input from you."

"Do I think I'm crazy? That's your question?" he nods. "If anyone's crazy it's my brother. Do you know that he has fifteen pillows on his bed? Fifteen. And he's not even married. Now that's fucking crazy doc." He has no response and I can tell that he is waiting for me to really answer the question. "I don't think I'm crazy doc. I'm just having a tough go at it. That's all."

"A tough go at what?"

"Life, I guess." My right leg begins to bounce up and down as the anxiety surfaces.

"What about life? What is so tough about it right now?"

I'm a little irritated now. "I don't know, it's life, it just sucks." My right leg is bouncing faster now and he notices it and glances at it and then looks back at me.

"What sucks about it?" He grabs his bottle of water that is in front of him on that tacky IKEA coffee table. He unscrews the cap and takes a drink. I look at my bottle of water that is in front of me but I'm not thirsty so I leave it alone.

"I don't know, what doesn't suck about it? All we do in life is wake up, go to work, eat a little, shit a little, and sleep. How does that not suck?"

"I thought you weren't working now."

"I'm not, but still."

"Ryan, your brother tells me that you have not left your room in over two months."

I am getting a little more irritated now. "That's not true." I shake my head. "That's not true doc, I ran out of toilet paper once and I had to go into his bathroom to get a roll." The doc looks at me like I'm fucking crazy, but I'm not, so whatever.

"Well besides that, why have you not left your room these past two months?"

"Where am I gonna go doc? I have no reason to leave. Besides it a nice room and the bed is awesome. It's one of those Sleep Number beds." We stare at each other again. My right leg is still going at it like a rabbit on cocaine. I nod my head as he thinks of what to say next.

"Fifty-five." I add.

"Fifty-five?" He says with a confused look on his face.

"That's my sleep number. Fifty-five." He looks at me like I'm looney tunes and continues with the inquisition.

"Well your brother told me that he believes you haven't left your room because your relationship with Shellie ended."

Hearing that name, the name that should not be said, punches me in the heart and I wince in pain. Now I am really irritated. The left leg joins the right.

"Please don't say that name doc."

"Okay, but can you at least tell me what you're feeling right now?"

I am fidgeting like mad, I comb my hair with my right hand and then I massage my neck.

"I'm irritated to be honest with you. I'm not too happy with where this conversation is going doc." I start biting my nails. I cross my left leg over my right, which mutes the bouncing.

"I'd like to know what happened between you two if you are up for it."

I am going at my nails big time now, like a wild fucking animal. "I don't think so doc. I'm really not ready to discuss that topic." I quit biting my nails and start pulling on the short beard hairs right below my lower lip.

"I would like you to try Ryan, at least say something about it, anything would suffice." He is staring at me hard.

"It's over. That's all that matters. No reason to dwell on the past, right?" I say with a smile, but he is not buying it.

"But you are dwelling on the past. You haven't left your room in over two months. I'm trying to help you not dwell on it Ryan. That is why you're here, right?"

"I'm here because my brother wants me out of his house. I don't wanna be here. I'm fine, I've just been in a funk that's all."

"Why have you been staying at your brother's house

Ryan?" I look up at the ceiling. "Ryan, why have you been staying at your brother's house and not your place?"

"I don't know. My place sucks and he has cable."

"Does it maybe have to do with the fact that you tried to kill yourself?"

"No." I shake my head. "That's not what happened doc. I didn't try to kill myself. I thought about it and then I called the suicide hotline to get some help; Big difference."

"And did you get help?"

"Yeah, I went down to the psycho clinic that night and they evaluated me and they gave me a prescription for some anti-depressants. Wellbutrin I think. Well, the generic version anyway."

"Are you still taking that medication?"

"Of course I am." I blurt out. "And Abilify."

"So you feel that you need to be on those meds?"

"Um Yeah."

"Why?"

"Well if I wasn't on them I would probably go fuckin' nuts."

"So you do think you're crazy?" Damn, he got me there. I take a few seconds to come up with my response.

"Well…I don't know…maybe." I look at the clock and he follows my eyes with his. I look back at him. "I'm depressed doc, okay? It's just a little depression."

"It says here that you were diagnosed with severe depression and then a moderate case of bipolar disorder a few weeks ago is that correct?"

"If that's what it says doc, then I guess that's what I have."

"What about that bandage on your forearm?"

I knew that question was coming. "What about it?" I shoot back defensively.

"I would like to know what happened…to your arm?"

"Well, I don't really want to talk about it."

"Well, I think we should."

I am pretty pissed off at this point and I can tell he is challenging me. "You want to know what happened doc?" I tear the bandage off and expose my scabbed up forearm. There are dozens of one to two inch cuts and together they are about three inches wide. "I cut myself okay. Are you happy now?"

"Why are you cutting yourself Ryan?

"Because I want to."

"Ryan, we both know that's not true. Tell me why."

I rub my head, take a deep breath, and exhale. "You want the truth doc?"

"Yes Ryan that is why we're here, to be truthful."

"Okay." I look at my scabbed over arm. "I cut my arm because feeling the pain of the blade going into my skin distracts my brain from feeling the other pain, the pain in my heart. The pain that beats me down every day and every night. For those few moments I'm free. And watching the blood run down my arm reminds me that I'm still alive and I like that. It's a great fucking feeling doc. That is why I cut myself." I place the bandage back over my scabbed up forearm.

At that moment the door to the room flies open and we both look over towards it.

"Are you two fucking done yet? It's one after eleven." A girl yells at us as we stare at her. Her hair is mostly light blond but parts of it are pink and purple. She has crystal blue eyes and a pierced nose.

"We are just finishing up Zoe, give us a couple of minutes."

She looks at me and rolls her eyes. "Whatever." She says as she slams the door shut.

"Sorry about..." the door opens again.

"And I'm not paying for the full hour Dr. Wagner just so you know." She looks at me again and slams the door shut again.

"Sorry about that, Zoe is very particular when it comes to being on time...among other things."

"You should ask her if she thinks she's crazy, but I think we both already know the answer to that question."

He ignores me. "So, I guess we can continue our conversation next week. What I would like you to do in the meantime is get out of the house, not permanently, but at least open the door and stand outside for thirty minutes or so each day. Can you do that for me?"

I roll my eyes. "Alright doc, you want me to get some fresh air, I'll get some fresh air."

"Thank you." Dr. Wagner stands up and I follow his lead. We shake hands and I walk to the door. When I open the door

Zoe is standing there blocking my way. We stare at each other.

"Excuse me." I finally say. She sneers at me and after a few seconds she moves to the side. I walk a couple steps and then look back towards her. She is still looking at me and rolls her eyes. I glare at her and then turn my head back around. I walk out of the office, down the hall, and enter the elevator, which is almost full. As the elevator doors close I say out loud to know one in particular "what a crazy fuckin' bitch." Everyone in the elevator looks at me like I'm crazy and I think to myself, maybe I am.

CHAPTER TWO

    I arrive right on time for my next appointment with Dr. Wagner, the shrink, Dr. Feelbad as I like to call him. As I enter the waiting room his nine o'clock patient exits his office as does he.

    "Ryan." He sees me right away. "Come on in."

    I continue on into his office and we take our usual seats. He is wearing another getup that makes me cringe. Plum dress shirt, pink paisley tie, grey slacks, and black dress shoes; again with the tassels. His socks, once again though, are awesome. They have thin horizontal stripes that go around them in every shade of purple imaginable. I decide to compliment him on his socks.

"I like those socks Doc, they're pretty sweet."

He looks down at them and then back up at me. "Thank you Ryan." He scans my attire trying to find something to compliment me on. "Is that a new haircut?" My outfit is the same as last week and he knows he would be a condescending prick if he said he liked my sweat pants.

"Yes it is. I did it myself. Number four on the sides and the back." I rub that area with my right hand. "Number nine on the top." I comb the top over with the same hand. "And then I just fade it together with the five and then the seven and boom, done."

"That's impressive. Not too many people can cut their own hair these days and make it look good."

"Yeah well I used to go get it done at a place back when it was eight bucks. But now it's like twenty bucks, if you include a tip, which I do because I hate people who don't tip, they should be murdered, literally." His ears perk up at that statement. "But anyway, twenty bucks for a haircut? You talk about crazy doc. That shit is crazy. You should leave some of your business cards at all the haircut places in town. Those crazy bastards need more help than I do."

He gets up, walks over to his mini-fridge, grabs two bottles of Fiji water, walks back over, and sets one on the tacky coffee table in front of me. He sits back down, sets his bottle of water on the table and begins the inquisition.

"So, did you get outside this past week like I asked?" He crosses his left leg over his right.

"I did. I sat out on the front porch for thirty minutes every day."

"And how was it?"

"It was nice. Very peaceful. Tranquil in fact."

"Did you see any people out walking or any animals roaming around?" That seemed like an odd question I thought.

"Yeah, I saw a few mothers pushing their kids in strollers and a couple of joggers."

"Any animals?" Damn, he knows.

"Did my brother call you?"

"Yes. A couple of days ago."

"Jesus Christ." I roll my eyes, annoyed.

"He was worried about you."

"Why? Because I was talking to a squirrel?" The doc nods. "Look, the squirrel came down from the tree, stopped on the lawn right in front of me, and stared at me for a good sixty seconds. I mean we literally locked eyes for a full minute. So I finally said "what are you looking at? And he ran off. The next day he came down again and then again the next day and so on."

"What would you say to him when he came to visit you?"

"Oh you know, whatever you would say to a person who came to visit you. What's up? How's your day? See ya later? Stuff like that." He is writing in his notebook. I sit up in my chair. "It's not a crazy thing doc. I was being friendly that's all." He finishes what he was writing and looks at me.

"It's fine. I don't really want to talk about the squirrel."

"Good, neither do I." I fall back into the chair, stretch my legs out, and cross them at the ankles.

"What I want to talk about today is your life before this past relationship."

"Okay. What about it?"

"I don't want to limit you to a particular set of questions. Just tell me whatever you want to tell me about it."

I look up at the ceiling and begin to stroke my beard. "Hmm…"

"You can tell me your life story if you want or you can talk about your station in life at that point, it's up to you."

"My station in life?"

"Yes. Your professional life, your personal life, how you were feeling, Were you happy? Sad? Depressed? Things like that."

"Well I don't want to bore you with my life story so…" He cuts in. "Like I said, whatever you want to talk about, but prior to your relationship with Shel-." He catches himself and I glare at him. "Sorry, I mean…you know who."

"Its okay doc…nice catch by the way." I uncross my feet and sit up a bit. "Prior to that whole thing I was good. I was single, employed, in good shape, not much else really. I wasn't depressed but I wasn't all happy go lucky either. I was just going through the motions of life I guess. Waking up, cup of coffee, going to work, coming home, a little exercise here and there, eating whatever. Life was okay."

"But something was missing?"

"Well yeah, of course. I wanted to find someone to love just like everyone does."

"Were you actively looking for someone? Dating? Socializing?"

"Not really. I mean I had a couple friends try to set me up with friends of other friends, the usual situation."

"How did those go?"

I laugh. "They went like they usually go, terrible. They would talk about their work and hobbies and all the blah blah blah bullshit you hear on first dates and it killed me. I hated it and decided after the third one to give it up and just stay single." I pull out my cellphone to check the time.

"You expecting a call?"

"No, just checking the time."

"Are you anxious to get out of here?"

"No, just curious." He looks at me like he doesn't believe me. I grab my bottle of water, twist off the cap, and take a drink.

"So, what's the longest relationship you've been in Ryan?

I look to the left at the wall, thinking about it. I notice the doc's diplomas, framed, hanging on the wall. Damn, this guy went to Columbia, nice. That explains the ridiculous outfits. I look back at him. "Um, two years exactly. To the day."

"Was this the last relationship?

I fidget in my chair and rub my head and face with my hands. "Yeah."

"So you're saying that it ended on the day of your second

anniversary together?"

"Yep, exactly two years to the day that we met." My mood changes from irritated to sad, depressed, no wait, more like melancholy, yeah, melancholy. The Doc notices this and checks his watch. Time is about up and I can see that he is trying to decide whether to press on or stop for the day.

"Can we call it a day doc?" I decide to try to make the decision for him.

"Well I would like to continue, but I don't think we have time to get into it. Plus I have Zoe scheduled right after you again and as you saw last time, she doesn't like it when I go over into her time."

My first thought was great I have to see that crazy chick again. "Well, until next time then I guess. Is there anything you'd like me to do this week?" I have no idea why I just asked him that. I stand up and he follows.

"As a matter of fact yes, I would like you to go for a walk every day, around the neighborhood, for say thirty minutes or as long as you feel like it. Is that okay?"

"Sure doc, I will give it a try. I could use a little exercise anyway."

We shake hands and I head towards the door. I open it and my body tenses up fully expecting to see Zoe standing there but she isn't. I exit the office and head down the hall towards the elevator. As I stand in front of the elevator doors waiting for them to open, a memory enters my mind. A memory I wish would fade away. The memory of the last time I saw you know who.

I was waiting for an elevator just like this and when it opened, there she was. She was wearing jeans and a t-shirt I had bought her at a Radiohead concert we went to several months prior. Her dark brown hair was put up in a ponytail exposing her long neck. I love necks, especially hers; it is the sexiest part of a woman's body. She made eye contact with me and smiled. I did not smile back. She had the cutest smile I had ever seen. I contemplated taking the next elevator but I decided not to. I wanted to stand next to her, smell her perfume, just one more time, crazy I know. I entered the elevator and stood next to her. As the elevator went down I contemplated whether to say something or not. I turned my head towards her and she turned her head towards me. She smiled again. I didn't smile back. I couldn't think of anything to say but I could tell that she wanted to say something, but she didn't.

The memory of that encounter left as quickly as a lightning strike when the elevator I am currently standing in front of dinged and opened. At that moment I am face to face with Zoe. Her light blond hair is pulled back into a ponytail and I notice the streaks in her hair are now blue and orange, my favorite color combination.

"Excuse me." She says in a bitchy tone. I'm staring at her neck now. "Hey, crazy, you're in my way." I look up at her eyes.

"What?"

She pushes me to the side and walks by. "Geez, what's wrong with you?" she yells as she walks down the hall. I'm still standing there and I turn my head and watch her walk away. When she enters the Doc's waiting room I turn my head back to the elevator, which is closed now.

"Fuck." I say out loud and then I decide to just take the stairs.

CHAPTER THREE

I'm running a little late to my third appointment with Dr. Wagner, AKA Dr. Feelbad, because the traffic today is ridiculous. It seems like every road and highway in the city is under construction and my road rage is out of control. I decide to try to calm myself down so I put my ear buds in, turn on my IPod, and scroll to Jack Johnson's *Sleep Through the Static*, which always helps me calm down. I pull into the parking lot five minutes after ten. I make my way up to the waiting room as quick as I can. When I get there the front desk girl tells me to go right in, Dr. Wagner is waiting for me. I enter his office and he stands.

"Ryan, glad you could make it." He says it in a nonsarcastic way and I get the impression that he is honestly glad to see me. And to be honest, I'm glad to see him.

"Sorry doc, traffic was a bitch." I take a seat in my usual chair. A bottle of Fiji water is already on the table in front of me. "Damn road construction doc, on literally every street."

"Yeah I know. You would think they would build them better the first time."

"Yeah, no kidding. That's what I always say." His outfit is typical but this time his socks are boring, just solid black.

"So Ryan, how was your week?"

"Um, not too shabby. Pretty low key."

"Really? Are you sure about that?" Damn he knows.

"I take it you talked to my brother again?"

"I did."

"What did he say this time?"

"He said you yelled at a little old lady that lives down the street from you."

"Well that makes me sound like an asshole. That's not what happened doc, there was more to it than that."

"Well tell me what happened then."

I run my right hand through my hair and then down to my neck and begin to massage it. "Well, I went for a walk around the neighborhood, like you asked me to. And on the third day, which I think was Sunday, I was walking by this house and this dog jumped off of its porch and started running towards me, barking. I didn't want to get bit so instinctively…I kicked it."

"You kicked it?"

"Yep."

"And then?"

"And then this little old lady comes running towards me from the same porch yelling and screaming. She knelt down, checked the dog out, picked it up, and then proceeded to spit profanities at me like a sailor. Then..."

The Doc interrupts me. "Wait. This little old lady picked up the dog? What kind of dog was it?"

"A Chihuahua I think, maybe a pug or a mix, I don't know it looked like a Chihuahua to me."

"A Chihuahua?" he shoots back, his eyes wide, and his tone surprised and disgusted you could say.

"Yep."

The Doc shakes his head. "You kicked a little Chihuahua dog?"

"It was vicious Doc. You should have seen the teeth on that little bastard."

"And what happened after she yelled at you?"

"She called the cops."

"And what did they do?"

"I don't know, I got the hell out of there and went back home. I guess they stopped by the house a little later and my brother talked with them. That's all I know."

"Maybe getting you to take a walk was a little premature on my part."

"Doc I would have been fine if that lady could have

controlled her dog."

He looks at me and I can tell he is trying to think of something to say in response. "Okay, well let's try not to kick any more dogs in the future, or anything for that matter, okay?"

"I can't promise you anything doc, but I'll try." And on that note he continues with the inquisition.

"So, on a different topic, I wanted to get into the subject of you know who today. How do you feel about that?" I lean back in my chair and start to fidget a bit, but not as much as I have in the past. I rub my head and face with my right hand. He can tell that the question has made me a tad uncomfortable. "Or not, if you're not feeling up to it…"

I sit up in my chair and look down at the ground for a few seconds. "No, I think I'm ready Doc. Let's give it a shot."

"Okay, great. Tell me how you two met."

I put my hands over my face and then sit back in my chair. Then I start to laugh. "It's so cliché Doc, it really is." I laugh again. "I was in front of the produce section at the supermarket staring at it with no idea what I looking for. I was just standing there holding one of those reusable grocery bags. Then I hear this girl's voice say, are you okay? I hesitated for a second and then turned my head and there she was. This beautiful girl with dark brown hair and green eyes was looking at me."

I stop as I feel tears begin to well up in my eyes but I fight them off. "I was mesmerized Doc. She was something else.

Then she asked me again if I was okay and I finally said, yeah
I'm fine. She asked me if I needed some help and I couldn't
answer her. I was just standing there like an idiot, staring at
her, but I finally said, help? And she said, yeah you look lost
in this sea of veggies." I smile and laugh a little as I remember
it. "I don't know why I remember that…Then I told her I had
no idea what I wanted and she asked me what I was making
and I told her I had no idea. Then I remember I asked her what
I should get and she went on for a bit about how serious that
question was and how she couldn't possibly tell me what to
get because she didn't know me. It was a bit odd, but I liked it.
Then she told me her name and I told her mine."

I close my eyes and I see the scene vividly in my head like
it was yesterday. "Then she made fun of me for using a
reusable grocery bag when I started to put the veggies in those
plastic bags you tear off. So I just threw the veggies into the
reusable bag. Then I remember this lady cut in between us to
get something and we just stood there, silent, staring at each
other, smiling. Then she asked me if I wanted to walk around
the store and finish shopping with her and I said yes and the
rest is history."

"So, it was love at first site for you then?"

"Yeah, well for both of us, at least I thought so." My right
leg begins to bounce as the anxiety surfaces.

"And so what happened?"

"What happened when?

"How did it the relationship end Ryan?"

I close my eyes and don't answer him.

"If you're not ready to discuss that part of it I understand."

I take a deep breath and exhale. "Just give me a second doc." He sits in silence and I finally reopen my eyes and answer him. "Well, on our two year anniversary we were having dinner at this Thai restaurant she loved, we loved, and she told me as we ate our chicken pad Thai." I sit up in my chair and put my hands to my face. I try to fight back the tears as Dr. Wagner presses on.

"Did she tell you why?"

"She said she'd met someone else and she was in love with him. It was a blindside job doc, I didn't see it coming. I thought we were great. In fact, I had a ring in my pocket and I was about to ask her to marry me before she dropped that bombshell on me. You can imagine my shock and why I am sitting here with you right now."

"That must have been extremely heartbreaking Ryan, I'm sorry."

"Yeah, well, what are you gonna do? You either piss it off and move on or you let it eat at you. And eat at me it did doc…and still does."

"That explains a lot Ryan and I am glad you shared that with me. Now we need to figure out how you can…to use your words…piss it off and move on."

"Well that's your job isn't it doc."

"Yes it is Ryan. Yes it is. But I was hoping that you could assist me."

"I guess. How?"

"Well, how do you think you can get passed this? How can we get you over Shellie?"

"I don't know. We could kill her?"

The doc tilts his head to the right and gives me one of those don't go there looks.

"And that asshole she's with." He tilts his head to the other side, the same look on his face. I smile. "I'm kidding doc. How about we kidnap her and force her to love me again?" He shakes his head. "I kid doc, I kid. I have no idea how to deal with it, which is why I've been locked up in my brother's guest room for three months."

"Do you still have anything of hers? Any clothes or trinkets? Any pictures?"

"Um, I have some pictures and the engagement ring I was going to give her the night she ended it."

The doc looks at me like a light bulb went off in his head. "You still have the engagement ring?"

"Yep. And some pictures."

He sits back and crosses his right leg over his left. "I understand the pictures, but why do you still have the ring?"

"I don't know. After she broke up with me I went home and set it down somewhere. Then a week or so later I threw it in a drawer and there it sits today."

"So you know where it is?"

"Yeah, as far as I know it's still in the drawer. Why?"

He sits up and leans forward placing his hands together

and resting them on his chin. "Can you bring it and all the pictures you have of her and anything else you might have that reminds you of her?"

"Sure, but why?"

"Just bring everything you have and we will discuss it next week. Okay?"

"Yeah sure doc."

"Okay, great. Well, time is up. I will see you next week."

"Sounds good doc."

We both stand and I head towards the door, Dr. Wagner follows behind. I open the door and right away make eye contact with Zoe, who is seated in the waiting room. She gives me the stink eye as Dr. Wagner tells her to come into his office. She gets up and as we pass each other her elbow brushes my forearm and I can smell her perfume, which smells like a combination of peaches and bubble gum. I don't look back as I hear Dr. Wagner's door close behind me. As I walk down the hall towards the elevators I realize I have smelled that perfume before and tears begin to well up in my eyes as I picture Shellie in the bathroom four months ago spaying that exact fragrance on her half-naked body.

CHAPTER FOUR

I wake up the morning of my fourth session with Dr.
Wagner and get out of bed after lying there for several minutes
contemplating if I could do what he had asked me to do. I had
not, up to this point, done any of it. The engagement ring was
still where I left it, in the top drawer of my dresser, where I
kept my socks and underwear. Most of the pictures I have of
Shellie and I are on my laptop, but I do have a small photo
album of pictures that she had given me on our one year
anniversary, which was on a shelf in my closet. I had lied to
Dr. Wagner, well not really lied just had forgotten, that I had
an article of clothing of Shellie's, a plaid mini skirt. It was the
only thing she left when she moved out. She hated that skirt,

mainly because I frequently asked her to wear it when we had sex. We got into a few arguments about that damn skirt and she left it on our bed when she moved out. But you know what? Every guy has their thing when it comes to sex, fetishes or whatever. So what if I got off on having sex with women while they wore a short skirt. And it didn't have to be a plaid school girl type skirt. It could be a denim skirt, or a leather skirt, or any kind of skirt, I didn't care. I have no idea why but that was my thing. Some guys like women to wear costumes or they have a foot fetish or they like to be spanked or whatever. I'm a short skirt guy, don't judge me, I like what I like.

After I took my morning piss I headed to my closet and grabbed the photo album off of the shelf and threw it on the bed. I stood there for a good minute trying to remember where I had put the skirt and then remembered that I had put it in the bottom drawer of my dresser. I walk over, squat down, and pull the drawer out and there it is, folded nicely, lying on top of an old t-shirt of mine. I grab it, stand back up, and toss it on the bed next to the photo album. I turn back around and face the dresser, staring at the top drawer, hesitant to open it, which is weird because I had opened it every day of my life to get socks and undies for the day. But this time I was getting something else out of it, something I wasn't sure I wanted to get rid of.

I remember back to that night, the night of our second anniversary, the night that was supposed to be one the greatest nights of my life, but turned out to be the worst. It's funny, but not really, how that happens, how life can take a complete one hundred and eighty degree turn in one split second. Just like death, one minute you are driving down the street and a second later, BAM! A truck T-bones you and you are dead, just like that. I have always tripped out on shit like that. This wasn't death, but it was the closest thing to it.

I remember her face when she told me that she had fell in love with someone else. It was one of those I'm sorry but I'm not looks. I could tell she was sad for me, for us, but that she was relieved to finally get it off of her chest and move on with her new life. I was like a deer in headlights. I was side-swiped and totally caught off guard, t-boned by a semi that looked like a pretty brunette. I sat there thinking back over the past two years and I could honesty say that I saw no warning signs, no gut feelings, no nothing that would ever make me think she was with someone else. She was never late and I couldn't remember her ever making an excuse to leave the house or cancel our plans. At one point I thought she might be making it up as a way to end our relationship, but it was later confirmed by a mutual friend of ours.

I snapped out of my daydream or day-nightmare I guess would be a more appropriate term when my cellphone rang. I walk over to my nightstand, pick it up, and see that it's Dr. Wagner calling. I hit the answer button.

"Hello."

"Ryan, this is Dr. Wagner. How are you?"

"I'm hangin' in there doc, just getting together the items you asked me to."

"Good, I'm glad you have the willingness to do this. So, I was thinking that instead of meeting at my office we could meet somewhere else. Is that okay with you?" I pause for a few seconds, thrown off by the request.

"Ryan, are you there?"

"Yeah doc I'm here."

"So, is that okay?"

"Yeah, I guess. Where do you want to meet?"

"Johnson Park. Same time we usually meet, which is in an hour."

"Okay doc, I'll be there."

"Great! And don't forget to bring the items we discussed."

"I have them right here." I look at the items on my bed.

"Okay, see you in an hour."

"See ya doc."

I hit the end call button on my cellphone and toss it on the nightstand. I turn and look at the photo album and skirt that I had thrown on the bed and then I look at the top drawer of my dresser. I take a deep breath and exhale. Then I walk over to my dresser, grab the nob of the top drawer, and open it. The drawer is filled with my socks on the right side and my underwear on the left side. Nothing is folded, just wadded up, but separated; I'm not a complete animal. I reach my hand into my clean undies and feel around towards the back of the drawer. I finally feel the small hard velvet box that contains the ring.

I grab it and remove it like a doctor removing a heart during surgery. I stare at the black velvet box but I can't open it. Tears begin to well up in my eyes but none slide down my face. I gain my composure and toss the box on the bed with the other items and then I head to my desk and get on my laptop. I drag the folder containing all of the pictures I have of Shellie into an empty flash drive I have in my desk drawer. Then I delete the folder, remove the flash drive from my laptop, and throw it on the bed with the other items. I shower real quick, get dressed, grab my backpack, throw the four items into it, zip it up, and head out of the room and the house.

When I arrive at Johnson Park I look around trying to locate Dr. Wagner but with no luck so I take a seat on a wooden bench and wait. I see him a few minutes later talking with a man next to his car. They are both wearing suits. Dr. Wagner's is grey and the other man's is navy or black I can't really tell from this distance. After a few seconds Dr. Wagner leaves the man there and starts to walk towards me. He is holding what looks like a plastic shopping bag in his left hand.

"Ryan. Good to see you." He says as he approached me. A huge smile is on his face. His suit bores me like it usually does.

"Doc, good to see you too. So who's the other suit?"

The doc looks back towards his car and then takes a seat next to me on the bench.

"That's a friend of mine. We'll talk about him a little later.

I take it the items I asked you to bring are in your backpack there?"

"They are. What's in your bag?"

"Follow me Ryan." He ignores my question as he gets up and I do the same. I follow him over to one of the picnic areas where he stops in front of a barbeque. It's one of those built-in charcoal grills you find at every park in every city in every state in America. "Ryan, one of the most important things we can do when it comes to putting things behind us is to get rid of the things that remind us of that painful past. This is an opportunity for you to do that. Can I have all of the photos you have in your backpack?"

I sort of knew that this was coming, but I hesitate as Dr. Wagner holds his hand out. "Ryan, if you want to get over Shellie and move on, you have to do this."

After a few more rebellious seconds I unzip my backpack and remove the small photo album and hand it to him. Then I reach back in and remove the flash drive that contains all of the other pictures from my computer and hand it to him. Then I reach back in a third time, grab the plaid skirt, and hand it to him.

"What is this?"

"That is a skirt." He looks at me funny. "I forgot I had it. She left it behind. She hated it."

"Okay. I don't think we need to get into that story. So, besides the ring is that everything you have of hers?"

"That is everything doc."

"Okay. I need you to throw those two things into the barbeque." I reluctantly do as he says. "Now I need you to remove all of the pictures in this photo album, tear each one in half, and then add it to the barbeque."

"Why?"

"It's part of the process Ryan. Trust me, there is a method to my madness."

I do what he says and I remove each picture and then hand him the empty photo album. I tear the first picture with the photo away from me and the doc tells me that I need to tear the rest while looking at the photo, which I am hesitant to do, but he again says it's part of the process. I do what he says and it is tough. I almost stop when I get to one of my favorite photos of us at a spring training baseball game, but I tear it in half after several seconds as tears well up in my eyes but never fall.

When I finish he takes a bottle of something out of his plastic shopping and hands it to me. I look at it and it's lighter fluid, one of those small yellow bottles one would use to refill a Zippo lighter. He tells me to douse the items with the lighter fluid, which I do after several rebellious seconds. I hand him back the lighter fluid and he hands me a small box of matches.

"When you're ready, just light a match and toss it in. This will cauterize the wounds that have been inflicted on you and it will allow you to begin the healing process. You're ready Ryan. Let the healing begin."

I stare at the matchbox for a few seconds and then open it.

I take a single match out and then close the box. I light the match, and after a couple seconds, I throw it in the barbeque, but nothing happens. The burnt match lays on a torn piece of a picture of Shellie in front of the penguin exhibit at the local zoo. I look at Dr. Wagner.

"Is that a sign doc?"

"No Ryan that was the wind." He says with a half-smile.

I take out another match, strike it, and then toss it into the barbeque. This time the items are engulfed in flames instantly and I look away.

"No Ryan. You have to watch it burn."

"Let me guess, it's part of the process?"

"Exactly, watch it deteriorate like the pain will deteriorate. Watch it disappear like the pain will disappear. And imagine a Phoenix rising from the ashes. You are that Phoenix. You will rise from the ashes of this stuff, this pain, and you will fly and soar and move on and love again."

I look at him like he's crazy and then I look back at the items, the memories that are quickly turning to ash. But all I can see is her. That smile and those eyes and tears begin to well up in my eyes. I can't stop them this time as they begin to slide down both of my cheeks. Dr. Wagner puts his right hand on my shoulder.

"It will be okay Ryan. You will get through this, I promise you."

"Can I leave now?" I say as I wipe the tears from my face with my hand.

"We have one last thing to do. Follow me."

He begins to walk away and I follow him. I look back at the barbeque and almost run back over to save what I can, but I don't. I turn my head back around and continue to follow Dr. Wagner. When we get to his car the man he was talking with earlier approaches us.

"Ryan, this is Steve, a good friend of mine. The man extends his right hand and I shake it as I wipe the remaining tears from my face with my other hand. "He owns a jewelry store downtown."

"It's nice to meet you Ryan."

I don't respond.

"I had him meet us here so he could take a look at the ring, appraise it, and hopefully buy it from you."

I look at the man and then I look at Dr. Wagner and then I look at my backpack.

"Is that okay Ryan?"

I squeeze my backpack for several seconds as the two stare at me and wait for my response. I relax the hold I have on it, unzip it, reach inside, and pull out the ring like death pulling out my soul when I die.

"Okay." I say as I hand the small black velvet box to Steve. He takes it from me and opens it.

"Wow, this is a very nice ring." He removes it from the tiny coffin it has been resting in for the past three months. I haven't actually seen the ring since that final night when I stared at it for a good sixty seconds just before I left to meet

Shellie at the restaurant.

Steve reaches into his left pant pocket and pulls something out and then he places it in his right eye. It is one of those magnifying eye things jewelers use to inspect gems or whatever. "This is a nice stone, the clarity is near perfect, and the color is nice." He removes the thing from his eye and continues to look at the ring. "The setting is beautiful too. Did you pick this out yourself?"

"Yep, well sort of. But every time we passed a jewelry store she would drag me over to look at the rings that were displayed and I just took mental notes every time so I knew what she wanted."

"You're a smart guy. Most of the men I deal with have no idea what they want."

"Well, I'm not that smart. If I was we wouldn't be standing here right now."

He looks at me with a sorry expression on his face and then he looks back at the ring. "I know this ring is probably priceless to you Ryan, but I can offer you two thousand for it."

This guy knows his rings. I paid twenty-four hundred for it. Money I had been saving since the day I met her. But it didn't matter anymore. It's not like I could just keep it and give it to the next girl, if there is even a next girl, it doesn't work like that. I had to sell it and Steve was giving me an honest price. It was time.

"It's not priceless Steve, it's a painful memory. I'll take the two grand."

"Great. Let me go to the car and get the cash." Steve closes the ring box, puts it in his front right pant pocket and then walks off. Dr. Wagner puts his right hand on my shoulder again.

"I'm very proud of you Ryan, this is not an easy thing to do. Now the healing can truly begin."

"It's time doc. It's time to get my shit together and try to move on." At that moment, for reasons unknown, I saw a vision of Zoe in my mind. It was from the first time I saw her in the doc's doorway as I was leaving his office. It wasn't a vision of her rolling her eyes or sneering at me. It was just her face, expressionless. Her hair, with streaks of pink and purple, put up in a quick ponytail. Her blue eyes, wide, as I stare at her. I close my eyes and when I open them it's not Zoe I am looking at, but Shellie, shaking her head.

"Here you go Ryan."

I snap out of it and the vision evaporates as quickly as it came. I look at Steve, who has his right hand extended, holding a white envelope.

I take it from him. "Thank you."

"No. Thank you." He says as we shake hands. He shakes Dr. Wagner's hand and tells him that he will see him Saturday for golf and then he walks back to his car and drives off.

"So what are you going to do with your new found fortune Ryan?"

I look at Dr. Wagner. "Vinyl doc." He has a confused look on his face. I place my left hand on his right shoulder.

"Records doc. I'm going straight to the record store and I'm gonna buy a shit ton of Vinyl records."

He smiles and nods his head. "I see, I didn't know you were into vinyl records."

"I love'em doc, absolutely love'em."

CHAPTER FIVE

I wake up three days later to the sound of someone knocking on my bedroom door but I ignore it. The banging continues, harder and louder now.

"Ryan, wake the fuck up!" I continue to ignore it. "If you don't open this door I'm gonna kick it in."

"Go fuck yourself Mitch." I yell back.

"I'm serious bro, open this goddamn door."

"Kick it in, I don't care, it's your fuckin' door, you're just gonna have to buy a new one anyway."

"If I have to kick this door down, it will stay down, and you will have to deal with not having a door."

That asshole knows me too well. "Alright, give me a

second." My room is a fucking mess. I haven't left it since I got back from the park after my last session with Dr. Wagner. There are vinyl records covering the floor and an ashtray overflowing with cigarette butts on the night stand next to my bed. It smells like an alley in Chinatown minus the food smell because I haven't eaten in three days. I've been surviving on cigarettes and sink water. I get out of bed and make my way slowly to the door, careful not to step on any of my records.

"You have three seconds Ryan."

I open the door. "Calm down. What do you want?"

My brother looks passed me into the room. "Judas priest, what the fuck have you been doing in here for three days? It smells like a dirty ashtray wrapped in a sweaty pair of boxer shorts."

"I don't smell anything." I am lying of course. He pushes his way in and looks at the floor.

"Jesus Ryan, can you pick this shit up?"

"Sure dad." He looks at me and shakes his head and then notices the cigarette butts.

"I thought I told you no smoking in the house man, shit."

"I opened the window dad I swear." He looks at me again and gives me the same look our dad had given us a million times.

"Will you stop calling me dad?"

"But you look just like him right now." He cracks a tiny smile and lets out a little chuckle.

"You dick." I shrug my shoulders. "Look man, I'm worried

about you. I thought things were going good with you. I thought your sessions with Dr. Wagner were helping."

I take a seat on the foot of the bed. "They are, well they were, I don't know. I don't want to talk about it right now."

He sits down next to me. "Well you look like shit man. When was the last time you ate something?"

"I don't know, Wednesday maybe."

"Jesus." He stands back up, walks towards the door, and turns around. "Do me a favor, clean up the records, take a shower, put on some clean clothes, and I'll go grab you a pizza. Cool?" I look up at him.

"Cool."

"Mushrooms, bacon, jalapenos, and pineapple?"

"Yep."

"Alright, I'll be back in thirty or forty minutes."

"I'll be here."

He turns and exits the room, closing the door behind him. I take a deep breath, my shoulders rise, and then I exhale as they fall back down. I get off the bed and begin to gather up all of the records that are scattered across the floor. Then I take the ashtray and empty it into the bathroom trash can. I grab the trashcan and set it outside my bedroom door, Mitch will take care of it.

Then I take a shower, a hot one, a nice one, the fiery water attacks my skin with ferocity, massaging me, loosening my aching shoulder and back muscles. It is the closest thing to an orgasm that I have had in four months. I turn off the water, exit the shower, and dry myself off. I get dressed in a pair of grey athletic shorts and a white V-neck t-shirt and lay on my bed waiting for my brother to return with my pizza. The hot shower has relaxed me so much, too much, and I feel my eyelids getting heavy.

I awake, again, to someone knocking on my bedroom door. It startles me and I jump up on my elbows. "I'm coming, hold your horses." I get out of bed, head to the door, and open it. "It's about..." I stop mid-sentence as I notice Dr. Wagner standing in front of me, holding a pizza box. "Dr. Wagner, what are you doing here?"

"Good afternoon Ryan. I was told you were a tad hungry." He says as he lifts the pizza box up towards me. I say nothing. "Can I come in?"

"Sure doc, why not." I take a deep breath and walk back to my bed. The doc follows and sets the pizza box on the bed. I sit on the bed, cross-legged. My brother walks in holding a chair in one hand and a few paper towels in the other. I give him a look and he shrugs his shoulders as he sets the chair on the floor next to the bed and tosses the paper towels on the pizza box. He walks back out and closes the door. I remove the paper towels from the top of the pizza box and open it. The smell is glorious.

"Hungry doc?"

"No thank you Ryan, I've already eaten."

I grab a slice and take a bite. It tastes better than it smells. The sweetness of the pineapple and the saltiness of the bacon and the kick from the jalapenos make my taste buds explode. The mushrooms and the cheese and the buttery garlic crust only add to awesomeness that is this pizza.

"So Ryan, what's been going on?"

"I didn't know you made house calls doc." I say, ignoring his question as I attack my first delicious slice of pizza.

"Well, your brother called me and said it was an emergency and that I should probably stop by, so here I am." I take another bite.

"Oh that brother of mine, he's a peach, isn't he?" I say as I continue to chew away.

"He cares about you Ryan. He's worried."

"Well he doesn't need to worry doc, I'm fine."

Dr. Wagner notices my record collection in the tall bookcase against the wall behind him. "So how did it go at the record store? Did you get some new vinyl?"

"Yeah, I got a ton of new stuff, well old stuff, but new to me." I finish my first slice of pizza and grab another.

"Really, what did you get?"

"Um…" I run my hand over the top of my head and begin to massage the back of my neck. "I got a couple Beatle records and some old punk stuff I have been looking for, The Clash, Sex Pistols, Ramones, stuff like that and a bunch of other stuff." I take a bite of slice number two.

"That's weird. I got call from my friend Steve, you know the jeweler who bought your ring, and he told me that you stopped by and tried to buy the ring back with the money he gave you."

"Really? He said that?" I take another delicious bite.

"He did." The doc crosses his left leg over his right and I notice his sock, which is bright neon green and I think to myself, damn this guy has great taste in socks, how can he have such terrible taste in shirts and ties? "That is weird." I say with a mouth full of pizza.

"Ryan, I can't help you if you're not going to be honest with me." I finish my bite and toss the unfinished slice of pizza back in the box. I take a deep breath, exhale, and begin to rub my eyes with my right hand.

"Look doc, I can explain."

"I would love to hear it."

"I did go to the record store after our meeting in the park. I was looking for a Blue Oyster Cult record that I have wanted for a while and..."

The doc cuts me off. "What record?"

His question throws me off a bit. "Huh?"

"What record was it?"

"Oh, *Tyranny and Mutation*. You know it?"

"No. I only know that reaper song, the one from that Saturday Night Live skit with Christopher Walken."

"Yeah, more cowbell. That's *Don't Fear the Reaper*, that's the song everyone knows. You should check out this record I'm talkin' about. There is this song on it called *7 Screaming Diz-Busters*. That shit is nuts doc, the fuckin' bees knees."

"I will give it a listen. So you were looking for this

record..."

"Yeah. So I find the B's and then I find the BL's and what is the first record I flip to? Fucking *Foiled* by Blue October and right when I flip to it what just happens to come on the store speakers? *Calling You* by guess who? Blue October." I look at him wide eyed like he is supposed to know what that means.

"And what is the significance of that song and that band?"

"It's Shellie's favorite band doc and even though I hate them, I like that song, that one fucking song that just happened to be playing at the exact moment I flipped to a record that was by that band, a different record mind you, but still. I mean are you kidding me, what are the odds of that doc? I mean come on." I am totally amped up right now.

"What did you take it to mean?"

"Well it was obviously a sign doc."

"A sign meaning what?"

"A sign that maybe it's not over, maybe there's a chance I can get her back. So I ran out of there and went to get the ring back."

"How did you know where the jewelry store was?"

"Steve put one of his business cards in the envelope with the two grand he gave me, which I believe was also a sign."

"I see. Well in regards to that I am sure he left his card because he is a business man and he wanted you to buy your next ring from him."

"Hmm." I think about that explanation.

"The other thing, the song thing, was just a coincidence Ryan. She is with someone else and there has been nothing that would suggest she wants to get back with you."

"Yeah I know." The doc is surprised by my comment.

"So you're giving up that easily?"

"Weeeeeell."

"Well what?"

"Well ya see doc the song is called Calling You so when I got back here after Steve wouldn't sell me back the ring I called Shellie.

"No you didn't?"

"Yeah I did."

"And what did she say?"

"She basically told me to fuck off. She said it was over. That we were through. And that she had moved on and so should I. Blah, blah, blah." I lie back on my pillow, take a deep breath, and exhale.

"So that is why you haven't left this room in three days?"

I smile, a big cheesy one. "Bingo."

"I think that's the first time I've seen you smile Ryan."

"It's a dolphin smile doc, don't get too excited."

"A dolphin smile?"

"Yeah, a dolphin smile, you've never heard that saying before?"

"I can't say that I have."

"Well, have you ever been to Sea World or an aquarium or any place where they have a dolphin show or tanks?"

"Sure"

"Well then you've seen them doing flips and jumping through hoops and shit."

"Yes."

"And they look like they're having a great time, they look like they're smiling, they look happy, but they're not. That smile was put there by Mother Nature or God or whatever. It's a fake smile and behind it is a sad, depressed, stressed out animal that just wants to be free. When I smile, it's a dolphin smile. I might look happy, but behind it... Well that's a story we both know all too well."

"Well let's work on turning that dolphin smile into a real human smile. Now finish up that pizza, you need to eat. I will see you in a few days for our scheduled appointment." Dr. Wagner stands up as do I.

"See ya doc." He opens the bedroom door and leaves, closing the door behind him. I sit back down and start in on the unfinished slice I tossed in the box earlier and think to myself, damn this is some good ass pizza.

ZOE

CHAPTER SIX

"So Zoe, how are you feeling today?"

I glare at Dr. Wagner, who is sitting there in his big stupid brown leather chair, wearing yet another pair of ridiculous looking socks. "I was fine until you decided to go over time with that crazy guy in the sweatpants."

"Now Zoe, what did we talk about last time? You can't go around calling people crazy. It's…" He pauses, thinking about what to say next, so I say it for him.

"It's like the pot calling the kettle black?" I say in a bitchy tone.

"No, that is not what I was going to say. It's just not appropriate. Its mean and a nice girl like you shouldn't be mean to people." I sit back as I roll my eyes and then start messing with my fingernails. "So, how are you feeling? Did you have a good week?"

"I feel the same as I always do Dr. Wagner and my week was the same as it always is." I start to pick at a small hole that is in the front right thigh of my jeans, which I bought that way. It has begun to fray a bit more and I find myself messing with it from time to time when I wear these jeans.

"Can you elaborate for me? Even if it was the same, I would like to know what you did." He grabs his notepad from the black table that separates us and then removes a pen from his left shirt pocket and clicks it open.

"I did the same as I always do, I slept for twelve hours and then I laid in bed for the other twelve."

"What about eating?" I look at him with a 'well duh' expression on my face.

"Okay, so I get out of bed to eat once a day, okay? Are you happy.?"

He looks at me with a slight look of annoyance on his face. "You should be eating more than once a day Zoe." He says with a concerned look on his face.

"Yeah I know and I should also not lie in bed all day. And I should also get out of the house more. And I should also be more social. And I should also not yell at everyone who annoys me. And I should not call people crazy. And I should get over my problems. And I should move on with my life. And I should be a happy little citizen who doesn't take meds, who doesn't cut herself, who doesn't try to kill herself, and who doesn't just lay in bed waiting for death to knock on the door. Right Dr. Wagner? That's about right, right?"

"Are you still having suicidal thoughts?"

"No. I'm over that."

"Good. We have made some progress then. Tell me again why you're over the whole suicide thing." I roll my eyes, extend my legs as I sink down in my chair, and then cross my legs at the ankles, left over right.

"You know why?"

"Humor me."

"You just want me to say it again."

"I do." After several seconds of staring at him in disgust I reluctantly say it.

"Fine, I will not kill myself because I have a purpose, I may not know what that purpose is yet, which I don't, but I have one and it's my job to live my life to fulfill that purpose."

"And?"

"And I don't want what's left of my family and friends to go through what I went through and am still going through."

"Good. Now we just have to work on your purpose. But we won't be able to do that if you don't do the things I ask you to do Zoe. You can't find your purpose if you don't leave the house. You won't find it lying in bed all day and sleeping all night…"

I cut him off. "It's actually in bed all night and sleeping all day."

"Whatever. The point is we have to get you going, you have to get yourself going. I can only help you so much. You have to take the initiative. Now let's figure out how we can get you going. Once you do that your purpose will present itself."

"And if it doesn't?"

"It will. You just have to believe that it will."

I close my eyes for several seconds and then open them. I sit back up in my chair and stare directly into Dr. Wagner's eyes.

"Okay, what do you want me to do?"

"Well, before we talk about that, let's talk about why you lie in bed all day or all night I guess it is. Is it fatigue? Is it lack of motivation? What do you think is the reason?"

I take a few seconds to think about the question. "I think it's a lack of motivation and possibly a fear of interacting with people. I mean I just wake up and I don't want to do anything. The thought of going somewhere and having to interact with people who are all happy-go-lucky makes me want to puke. When I am out in the real world I feel alone, like no one understands what I went through and what I am going through now. So I just lie in bed and do nothing."

"Do you really just lie there and do nothing?"

"Sometimes, well most of the time I guess. I mean sometimes I'll watch a movie or read a book, but most of the time yeah I just lie there."

"And what are you doing when you just lie there? Are you thinking about something or…" He waits for a response.

"Yeah I think about stuff. I cry sometimes too. Sometimes I just space out and there is nothing, I just stare at the ceiling not thinking about anything."

"When you do think about stuff, what kind of stuff do you think about?"

"The usual. My parents. My brother. My purpose too I guess."

"Losing a family member, let alone three of them in a short period of time, is a tough thing to deal with Zoe. Your actions are not unusual, they are actually typical. The pain you feel and have felt is excruciating and sometimes intolerable. I've lost a child, years ago, a still birth. It messed my wife and I up pretty bad, but we got over it and moved on with our lives. We had two amazing children after that, but if we had given up on having kids our two boys would have never been born. Looking back on it that would have been worse than anything else I could imagine. We take the bad stuff, we deal with it, and then we move on. Now I know you can't replace a mother or a father or a brother, but you have to figure out something else to replace it with."

I stare at him as my annoyed look turns into a sad one. Tears well up in my eyes and then slide down my cheeks. "I know Dr. Wagner, I know, but I'm not sure I'm ready."

Dr. Wagner hands me a box of tissue. I remove one and wipe away the tears from my face and then my eyes. "I have helped a lot of people Zoe and I know you are ready, you just have to trust me and the process."

I take another tissue and wipe my nose. Dr. Wagner writes something in his notepad.

"So what's the plan?" I ask him, still wiping my nose.

"Well, we have to get you out of bed and out of the house."

"I was afraid you were gonna say that."

"Let's start off with thirty minutes a day. Just sitting outside, you don't have to go anywhere or talk to anyone, just sit and relax."

"Okay Dr. Wagner, I can do that."

"We also need to get your sleeping back on track so if you're going to sleep twelve hours a day you need to sleep from midnight to noon. So set an alarm for noon and wake up then, even if you don't get to sleep by midnight, okay?"

"Okay." I set the box of tissue and the used tissues on the black table that is in-between us.

"Well it looks like our time is up. I will see you next week and remember to get outside for at least thirty minutes a day and get that sleep back on track."

"I will Dr. Wagner."

We both stand and I walk towards the door as he follows. I open the door and walk out.

"Have a good day Zoe."

"Same to you."

I walk out of the waiting room and head towards the elevators.

CHAPTER SEVEN

Dr. Wagner opens the door to his office from the inside and we lock eyes.

"Zoe, come on in." He says with a huge stupid smile on his face. I toss the Cosmo magazine I was flipping through on one of the tables in the waiting room and then stand up. I walk into his office and take a seat in the same chair I always do. Dr. Wagner takes a seat in his big stupid leather chair and looks at me with that same stupid smile plastered on his face.

"It's really great to see you Zoe, how was your week? I hope you ventured outside like we discussed last week?" He raises his eyebrows.

"Yes, Dr. Wagner I sat outside every day this past week for

thirty minutes like we discussed."

"And?"

"And it was okay."

"What did you see?

"What did I see? I don't know. I saw cars drive by and people walk by and a couple squirrels chasing each other around a tree." Dr. Wagner chuckles. "What?"

"Oh nothing. That just made me think of a conversation I had with the patient that was in here right before you."

"That guy in the sweatpants?

"Yeah."

"What was so funny?"

"You know I can't talk to you about another patient Zoe."

"Oh yeah I forgot." I remember what I said to that guy as I was getting off the elevator and I have a sudden case of guilt. "Speaking of that guy, I have a little confession to make."

Dr. Wagner crosses his right leg over his left and I notice he is wearing yet another pair of ridiculous socks. This time they are these hideous multi-purple colored striped socks.

"Oh yeah, what's the confession?"

"Well when the elevator opened he was standing there like a zombie, just zoned out, and he was in my way so I said, excuse me, and when he didn't move I called him crazy and then pushed passed him."

"Did he say or do anything?"

"No. At least I don't think so."

"Well I'm glad you told me, at least you're recognizing

when you are being not so nice to someone."

"Yeah, I kinda feel bad about it, but he was just standing there, staring at me. He needs help Dr. Wagner."

"I'm working on it Zoe."

"Can you at least tell me his name?"

"I guess that would be okay. His name is Ryan."

"Hmm"

"So Zoe, did you get your sleep schedule back on track? Did you wake up at noon like I asked you to?"

"Yeah, except for the day after I saw you. I set the alarm for noon but I was so tired, because I couldn't get to sleep until five in the morning, and I just turned it off and went back to sleep for a couple more hours. But the day after that I woke up at noon, I was still tired but I battled through it."

"Yeah it takes a day or two of being tired to get back on schedule. So besides sitting outside for thirty minutes each day, did anything else exciting happen this week?"

I sink down in my chair. "No, when I was finished outside I just went back to bed and did the usual."

"Hmm. Well, this week I would like you to take a thirty minute walk around the neighborhood, is that okay?"

"Yeah I guess I can do that."

"Great. Now, I wanted to end our session today talking about why you avoid people and social situations."

"Okay." I stare at him.

"So, you want to tell me why?"

"I don't know. When my dad and brother died I had my

mom, but when she died I was all alone. I just didn't know how to deal with it. I didn't know how to function, so I just stayed home. At first I went out only to eat or buy groceries but I just couldn't function in public. It was too uncomfortable, so I started having my groceries delivered, and then I never left the house until I started seeing you."

"What was it about being in public that made you uncomfortable?"

"People just annoyed me and they still do by the way. They are always smiling and saying hello and just being nice and I hate it. Why are they so happy when I'm so miserable? Why can't I be like them? Why can't I just live without being in so much emotional, mental, and physical pain? I didn't like feeling like that so I became a recluse and it made me feel better."

"But did you really feel better or did avoiding people just make life easier?"

"I don't know I guess easier is a better way to put it."

"Do you believe that everyone is really happy Zoe or is that just what you're seeing?"

"Look Dr. Wagner, I know everyone isn't happy, but when you deal with people in public, a waiter at a restaurant, a cashier at the supermarket, they are all smiling because that's part of their job. They could be going through the same thing I am, but they have to put on a fake smile and deal with it."

"So why can't you put on a fake smile when you go out and deal with it that way?"

"I guess I could, but would that really solve my problems?"

"Not all of them, but it could solve the problem of your anti-social behavior. When you go for your walks this week why don't you give it a try? When you pass someone on the street smile and say hi or if you see someone on their porch just give them a little smile and a wave, see what happens. Can you try that?"

"Yeah, I can give that a try I guess."

"But you're right Zoe that is not going to solve the problem. It is definitely a quick fix, but it's just a piece of the puzzle, a step in the process. Soon enough the rest of your problems will be fixed and that fake smile will be replaced with a genuine one."

"I hope so Dr. Wagner. I really hope so."

"Now, I noticed that you are not wearing any bandages this week. When was the last time you cut yourself?"

I look away from him and don't answer.

"Zoe, how long has it been?"

I take a deep breath and then exhale. I reach down and pull my left pant leg of my jeans up and expose a three inch by three inch tan colored Band-Aid. Dr. Wagner looks at it and then looks at me.

"You're still cutting?" he says and I can see the disappointment on his face.

"I hadn't done it in two weeks Dr. Wagner, but something happened and I just didn't know how else to handle it."

"What happened?"

I let go of my pant leg and shake it back down. "I was going through a storage box in the garage looking for my high school yearbook from senior year and I came across an old videotape that had Christmas 1999 written on it in green and red Sharpie. So I watched it on our old VHS player that we still have in the guest room and I lost it. I knew what was on it and I still watched it." I begin to cry and as the memory of what was on that tape fills my mind I cry even harder, covering my face with my hands.

Dr. Wagner gets up, walks around to me, grabs the tissue box off the table, kneels down beside me, and puts his hand on my right shoulder. "It's okay Zoe, its okay." He pulls a couple of tissues from the box. "Here, take these." I remove my left hand from my face and take the tissues from him and then place it back on my face. "Let me give you a few minutes, I will be back." He stands up and walks towards the door, opening it and then closing it after he exits. I try to shake the memory from my head and slowly but surely it fades away. I wipe the tears from my eyes and then blow my nose into the tissues. I toss the used tissues on the table with the other ones and sit there trying to compose myself.

"God, I'm a fucking mess." I say to myself out loud just before there is a soft knock on the door and Dr. Wagner opens it slowly.

"Can I come in?"

"Yeah, it's your office."

He enters and hands me some water and I take a drink. He kneels down and puts his hand on my shoulder again.

"I think that will do it for today. Its lunch now and I don't have any patients for a couple hours so you can leave when you're ready." He walks back over to his chair and sits down. "Next time you feel the urge to cut Zoe, you call me, I don't care what time it is, you call me okay?"

"Okay."

"And don't forget, thirty minute walks around the neighborhood this week and let's try to wake up at eleven this week also, okay?"

"Okay"

He stands up and leaves the room. After a good ten minutes I am fully composed so I stand up and leave. When I exit Dr. Wagner's office I see him talking to his secretary and they both look up at me. They both smile and I smile back.

"Was that a real smile?" He asks.

"Nope. Fake." I say as I walk through the waiting room towards the door.

"Well that's a start. See you next week Zoe."

"See ya Dr. Wagner."

I exit the door and make my way down the hall towards the elevators.

CHAPTER EIGHT

I get to Dr. Wagner's office a little early so I decide to stop at the Starbucks next to his building and get something to drink. I enter and head towards the register, passing displays selling everything from bags of coffee to coffee mugs to coffee makers and other accessories. There are two people in line in front of me so while I wait I peruse the menu on the wall behind the registers. When it's my turn, I smile, a fake one, and the girl behind the counter smiles back, probably a fake one too.

"What can I get started for you today?" she says in this uppity mousy voice. She is probably twenty years old and a sophomore at the junior college down the street. Her hair is up in a ponytail and I notice her nails are painted bright neon green. I hate her.

"I would like a grande iced vanilla latte with extra fat please." She has the look of a deer in headlights, frozen. I can hear the gears turning in her half-empty head.

"Did you say extra fat?" Her expression is priceless.

"You know what, I am trying to lose a few pounds, bikini season is right around the corner as you know. Let's skip the extra fat today and just go with a regular grande iced vanilla latte."

"Oh, okay." Still confused, she writes my order on a clear plastic cup. She apparently has no sarcasm radar. "And what is your name?"

"Zoe." She writes my name on the clear plastic cup and passes it off to another employee who begins making my iced coffee.

"That'll be four seventy-five." I hand her a five and she gives me a quarter back. I toss it into the tip container and smile, a fake one. "Have a great day." She says, still smiling. I'm pretty sure it's a goddamn genuine smile too; I hate her even more now.

A couple minutes later my name is called and I grab my iced coffee and take off towards the door. When I get outside I notice that she spelled my name Z-o-o-e-y and I hate her even more now. My name is not Zooey I say to myself. I don't live in a fucking zoo, ugh.

I head to Dr. Wagner's building, enter the main lobby, and

jump on the elevator. I get off on the third floor and head down the hall towards his office. I enter the waiting room and head to the front desk to sign in. I notice I still have five minutes until it's my turn. I take a seat and finish my grande iced vanilla latte. I get up and toss it into the trash can that is by the door and then sit back down.

I check the clock and notice that it's one minute to eleven and I start to get a little agitated. Dr. Wagner knows I hate it when people are late or run over into my time, but just as the clock is about to strike eleven his door opens and Mr. Sweatpants exits. He looks directly at me and I give him a dirty look, I'm not sure why, just habit I guess. I get up and as we pass each other I purposely brush him with my elbow and look back at him but he doesn't look back at me so I turn my head back around and enter Dr. Wagner's office.

Dr. Wagner grabs a couple waters from the mini fridge in his office and sets them down on the black table that separates our chairs and then sits down.

"So Zoe how was your week? Did you take your thirty minute walks around the neighborhood like I asked you to?"

"My week was okay and yes I took the walks."

"How about the eleven a.m. wake-ups?"

"Yes Dr. Wagner I did that too. You do know that I have to get up at nine in the morning once a week to make it here on time?"

"Yes Zoe, but that doesn't count?"

"Why not?"

"Because you don't sleep, you stay up all night and then go to bed when you get home after our session."

"You know me too well Dr. Wagner." I say with a smile.

"Was that a genuine smile I just saw?"

"Nope. Fake. Super fake in fact."

He cracks a little smile and chuckles a bit. "So anything interesting happen on any of your walks?"

"Interesting like how?"

"I don't know. Did anything stand out? You didn't kick any small dogs did you?" I look at him with a confused look on my face, not too dissimilar from the look the Starbucks girl gave me not twenty minutes ago, yet very dissimilar. "Sorry, I just can't get the image out of my head."

"Dr. Wagner did you kick a small dog?"

"Me? Oh God no. It was another patient of mine, forget it."

"Oh my God it was Mr. Sweatpants wasn't it?"

"Zoe you know I can't talk about other patients with you or anyone for that matter. And his name is Ryan, not Mr. Sweatpants."

"See it was him. He kicked a dog? A small one? What kind was it? Why did he kick it?" I am like a five year old who just found out about something really cool like rollercoasters or trampolines.

"Zoe we need to talk about you, not Ryan. Now did anything interesting or noticeable happen on any of your walks?"

I sit back in my chair and try not to think about that Ryan

guy kicking a small dog for some reason but it's hard not to.

"I don't know let me think about it for a second. Okay I did see two squirrels chasing each other around a tree and right when I was walking by them they both stopped and looked at me." Dr. Wagner started to chuckle again. "What now, did he kick a squirrel too?"

"No he didn't kick a squirrel Zoe. Continue."

"Ah, come on Dr. Wagner that's not fair."

"Just continue Zoe, anything else happen?"

"No, nothing that was unusual."

"Did you pass anyone and smile at them?

"Yeah, twice I think. Both were fake smiles, theirs were real I guess, but you never know."

"Exactly Zoe that's my point, you never know what other people are going through but yet they smile. It might be fake, but it doesn't matter. Hell most smiles that people give are probably fake, that's just how it is."

"Yeah I guess, but I would like to smile for real one of these days."

"You will Zoe, you definitely will, just give it time."

"Time is all I have Dr. Wagner. I have plenty of time."

"You can't force it either, it will come when it comes, probably when you least expect it." He grabs his bottle of water off of the table and takes a drink and I do the same. "So Zoe let's talk about something a little different."

"Okay."

"What are your plans for the future? What do you want to

do with the rest of your life? Like for work?"

"I don't know that's a great question. I haven't really thought about it."

"Well you're going to have to think about it sooner than later. That life insurance money and court settlement cash is going to run out eventually."

"That is true. I don't know. Maybe I'll go back to school and finish college or something."

"That sounds like a great plan. I can help you with that if you need it."

"Yeah, maybe. I don't know. That seems so far away."

Dr. Wagner has a look on his face like a light bulb just went off in his head. "I have a great idea, your next assignment."

I look at him and think to myself oh great what now. "And what is that?"

"I want you to find a part-time job."

"What was that?" I say even though I heard him loud and clear.

"Find a part-time job. It will give you some extra cash and it will help you interact with people and you might even make some new friends. What do you think?"

"I think you need therapy Dr. Wagner. I'm not sure I'm ready for that."

"You are ready Zoe. It's the perfect next step in the process. You are progressing so well and I think this will be the thing that makes you turn the corner."

"I don't know. Let me think about it, okay?"

"Sure Zoe, take a week and think about it. In the meantime I want you to spend an hour a day this week interacting with people. You can walk around the mall or spend an hour at a park, something like that, okay?"

"Ugh, okay." I say like a five year old that was told she could watch T.V. but only if she eats her broccoli.

"And I want you to set your alarm for ten, okay?

"Okay Dr. Wagner, geesh."

"Well time is up. It has been a pleasure like always." He stands as do I.

"So what kind of dog was it?"

"Zoe, it's not going to happen so just drop it."

"Ah, come on Dr. Wagner."

"No way." He raises his right arm basically saying there's the door and I make a pouty face and walk towards it. I open the door and walk through, Dr. Wagner follows. As I am about to open the waiting room door which leads to the hallway I hear Dr. Wagner say "A Chihuahua." I turn around.

"What?"

"It was a Chihuahua."

My mouth drops open. "A Chihuahua?" He nods his head and I shake mine. "See ya next week Dr. Wagner."

"See ya Zoe."

As I walk down the hall towards the elevators I am still shaking my head. "Why the hell would he kick a Chihuahua?" I say out loud to myself. And I think I have got to find out about that and whatever happened between him and a squirrel. I am intrigued by this Ryan guy now and I decide to make a mental note that I will do whatever it takes to find out.

CHAPTER NINE

I'm awakened by an incoming call on my cellphone that is plugged in on the night stand next to my bed. I roll over and try to grab it, which is difficult because my eyes are not fully open and my vision is blurry. I finally get a handle on it with my right hand and rub my eyes with my left hand so I can see who is calling. It's Dr. Wagner and it's five minutes before nine in the morning. I debate whether to answer it or not, but decide it must be important so I hit the answer call button.

"You woke me up five minutes early Dr. Wagner, you better be in dire peril or something."

"No Zoe I'm not in dire peril, I just wanted to see if you could meet me at Johnson Park for our session today. I'm meeting Ryan there at ten for our session and I thought it would be a nice change of pace and you can count it as your hour outside today. What do you think?"

I stretch my legs and my left arm as I lay on my back in bed. "Okay Dr. Wagner, that sounds good. See ya in a couple hours."

"Great, see you then. Oh and I will meet you in the main parking lot."

"Okay, bye Dr. Wagner."

"Bye Zoe."

I hit the end call button and toss my cellphone back on the night stand and then stretch my entire body, legs towards the foot of the bed and my arms above my head, extending up the wall above my headboard. I relax and my arms fall to my sides. My first thought is that that Ryan guy will be there and I get the great idea that I will go to the park early and see what he and Dr. Wagner are up to. The alarm on my cellphone goes off as I sit up and slide my legs off of the side of the bed. I grab my cellphone, slide the alarm off, and then set it back down on the night stand.

I stand up and head towards the bathroom to shower. I turn on the water in the shower and then head to the sink while the water warms up. I undress and look at myself in the mirror. "God I'm disgusting." I say out loud to myself and I survey my face and body. I am not really disgusting, but I am thin, pale, and I have massive split-ends. I also have scars on my arms and legs from all the cutting. The bathroom begins to steam up and I head to the shower and hop in. The water feels amazing, it's hot, but not to the point of scalding hot. It batters my back and shoulder muscles almost to the point of pure unadulterated ecstasy. I wash my hair and then my body and as I do a vision of Ryan enters my head. It was the first time I saw him, well actually the second time I saw him, when he opened the door after his session with Dr. Wagner and we stood there looking at each other. My thought at that moment was wow he has amazing crystal blue eyes, but I play it off like I could care less about him.

That is what I do with guys. I pretend that I don't like them, even if I don't know them. Why? I don't know, I guess because if they like me I want them to come after me and if I'm mean to them and they still come after me, then they must really like me. I don't want to come off as some easy, slutty girl who is all goo goo gaga over a guy. I've been like that and guys will abuse it and just use me for sex and then dump me. I guess being a bitch up front is my defense mechanism when it comes to guys.

I turn off the shower and grab my towel. As I begin to dry off I realize that I haven't dated anyone since the death of my father and brother, which was a little over a year ago. God, I haven't even had sex since then either, ugh. But that's cool, the last thing I've thought about is guys or sex for that matter, until recently that is. This Ryan guy intrigues me no doubt. I really want to know, more like need to know actually, why he kicked a Chihuahua dog and what the hell happened between him and a squirrel. It has been gnawing at me for a week now. But how am I going to find out? I'm going to have to talk to him that's a given and I can't let him know that Dr. Wagner said anything. I don't want him to get in any trouble.

When I finish drying off I throw on some underwear and a pair of jeans. Then I put on a cute little pink bra and cover it with a Rolling Stones t-shirt. I finish off the ensemble with a pair of blue and green plaid socks and my low top black Chuck Taylors. I go back to the bathroom and throw my hair into a ponytail and then head to the kitchen to grab a quick bite to eat.

I toss two slices of whole wheat bread into the toaster and push the level down. While that cooks or toasts or whatever I grab a banana and peel it as I walk over to the pantry. I open the pantry door and look around for the honey, which I find and grab. I close the pantry door with my butt, because my hands are full, and walk back over to the toaster. I set the honey on the counter in front of the toaster and take a bite of the banana. At that moment the toast shots up and startles me to the point that I actually jump back a bit just like I did when I was a kid and my dad would do that Jack-in-the-box clown thing to the tune of pop goes the weasel, which I still hate.

I grab a paper towel and carefully take the two slices of toast out of the toaster and set them on the paper towel. I grab the honey, open the lid, and attempt to squeeze it onto the toast. Honey is such a bitch to get started. You have to be a super patient person to put honey on things and I am definitely not that person. I finally cover the toast with honey and scarf it down after I finish my banana. I toss the banana peel and the crumb riddled paper towel in the trash can and then head out the door.

I get to Johnson Park a little after ten and start looking for Dr. Wagner and Ryan. I spot them sitting on a park bench near the picnic area. I stand behind a tree so they can't see me but I'm far enough away that they probably wouldn't notice me if I was out in the open. After a little while they stand up and head toward one of the barbeques. When they get there Ryan grabs some things from the backpack he has with him and hands something to Dr. Wagner. Ryan tosses the things into the barbeque and Dr. Wagner hands something to Ryan that he took out of the plastic shopping bag that he is carrying. Their bodies are sort of in the way so I am not sure what is going on until flames explode from the barbeque. I assume that Dr. Wagner has made Ryan burn some stuff but I have no idea what and I am further intrigued as to who this guy is and what his issues are.

After several minutes they leave the ash riddled barbeque and head to the parking lot where they start talking to another guy. Ryan hands him something and the guy looks at it. The guy puts something to his eye and examines whatever Ryan has given him, which I assume is some sort of jewelry, a ring maybe. This is driving me crazy and I have this intense need to know what is going on and really who this Ryan guy is and why he is seeing Dr. Wagner. It has literally become an obsession now. The guy walks away and then returns and hands Ryan an envelope. Then the guy leaves and Ryan and Dr. Wagner talk for a few minutes before Ryan leaves. I decide to walk over now to start my session with Dr. Wagner.

"Where is he off to?" I say to Dr. Wagner whose back it to me. He turns around and smiles at me.

"Zoe, there you are, good to see you, how have you been?"

"Dr. Wagner, good to see you too, I have been fine, so where is he off to?"

"Who? Ryan? He's off to some record store I guess. Let's head over to that bench and talk a bit." He points to the bench that I saw him and Ryan sitting out earlier.

"Why?"

"Well I thought sitting would be more comfortable."

"No, why is he going to a record store?" I nod my head toward the direction Ryan left.

Dr. Wagner looks that direction. "I assume to buy some records."

"Who buys records anymore? Doesn't he have an IPod?"

"I don't know, I guess he just likes records. Why the sudden interest in what Ryan is doing?"

"I don't know, just curious I guess."

"Well you know what happened to the curious cat."

"I do?"

"Don't you?"

I shake my head. "No."

He gives me this I don't believe you look. "You've never

heard the saying curiosity killed the cat?"

"I have not. Wait, are you saying I'm going to be killed because I'm curious? That's not very nice Dr. Wagner."

"It's just a saying Zoe, relax. Let's go have a seat and talk."

"Okay." We walk over to the bench and take a seat.

"So Zoe, tell me about your week, where did you spend your hour a day?" I am looking towards the parking lot in a trance. "Zoe!" The trance shatters and I look at Dr. Wagner.

"What?"

"Are you okay?"

"Yeah, my mind is just a bit preoccupied at the moment."

"Preoccupied with what?"

"Oh nothing."

"Zoe, does this have anything to do with Ryan?"

"Who?"

"You know who."

"Mr. Sweatpants? Not at all."

"You are not a good liar young lady."

"Alright, you caught me. It's just that he intrigues me. I don't know why. I mean the kicking the dog thing and the squirrel thing, whatever that was, and the burning stuff." I stop talking, realizing that he wasn't supposed to know that I saw that and the look on his face confirms that.

"Were you spying on us Zoe?"

"Spying is such a serious word Dr. Wagner. I got here a little early and I saw you guys over by the barbeque and I was just observing, not spying, observing, that's a more accurate word for it." I smile, another fake one.

"I shouldn't have said anything last week that was my fault. You need to forget about Ryan and worry about what is going on with you."

"Dr. Wagner, I believe things happen for a reason. I believe your little slip up was supposed to happen."

"What do you mean?"

"I don't know, like I'm supposed to be intrigued by this guy, like I'm supposed to get to know him for some reason."

"Hmm. That's an interesting insight Zoe. Are you attracted to him? I mean is this a romantic thing or just a curious, who is this guy thing?"

"Well it's mainly a curious who is this guy thing, but he is cute so I guess it's a little bit of that too."

"I see. This is interesting now that I think about it." Just like last week, Dr. Wagner gets this look like a light bulb went off in his head. "I have a crazy idea. Remember last week when I told you, you should find a job?"

"Yeah." I give him a go on, what are you getting at look.

"Well what if you got a job at a record store and if fate is part of this whole thing then he will come in at some point and well there you go."

"Hmm. Is this your way of tricking me into getting a part-time job Dr. Wagner?"

"No, well yeah sort of I guess. It's more of a way for you to not only work and be more social and make some money, but to maybe get to know Ryan outside the brief run-ins you two have at my office."

"I like it. It's brilliant Dr. Wagner. But how do I know which record store he goes to?"

"Well there can't be that many and he doesn't drive so if it was me I would find the one closest to this park and try there first."

"What if they're not hiring?"

"You're a cute girl Zoe, I'm sure there's a store that can find you a few hours a week to work."

"Okay, I guess I can give it a shot."

"Sounds good. Now let's talk about you while we still have some time left."

"Okay Dr. Wagner, shoot."

"Okay well back to my earlier question, where did you go for your hour walks this past week?"

"The park by my house mostly, well every day actually."

"And what did you do?"

"I walked around a bit, sat on the grass by the small lake and watched the swans float around and the other birds flying around a bit. A couple times I brought a blanket, laid it down on the grass, laid on it, and just stared up at the sky watching the clouds, trying to see if any of them looked like animals or whatever. It was very peaceful."

"Were you thinking about anything during those times?" I look at Dr. Wagner like he caught me doing something wrong. "What was it?" With slight hesitation I answer him.

"I was thinking about Ryan and the dog and the squirrel, mostly."

"Oh good lord Zoe. This is all my fault. I'm a terrible psychiatrist."

"No you're not. You're the best Dr. Wagner. Remember this was meant to happen, I believe that with all my being."

"Just make sure you don't tell him that I told you about the dog kicking incident or the squirrel thing."

"Okay, well you didn't really tell me about the squirrel thing."

"That's true but still."

"I won't say anything Dr. Wagner. I will get it from him another way."

"Okay, good luck with that." He stands up. "Let's take a short walk to finish up."

"Okay." I stand up and we begin walking through the park.

"So I have to ask, any cutting this week?"

"No actually. I haven't cut since the last time when you saw my leg."

"That's good."

"Honestly, the thought of cutting hasn't even crossed my mind lately."

"That's really great Zoe. Hopefully you're done with all of that."

"I think so. At least I hope so."

"You are progressing very well Zoe. I am very proud of the progress you are making."

"Me too."

"Are you eating enough?"

"Yeah, I mean I'm not eating a ton, but enough to get me through the day without being fatigued."

"That's good to hear."

We walk for a few minutes later and make our way back to the parking lot where we say our goodbyes and until next times. Dr. Wagner offers me a ride home but I decline. He gets in his car and drives off and as he does I say to myself out loud. "Okay, now where are those fucking record stores?"

CHAPTER TEN

I walked around the neighborhood near Johnson Park but never found the record store so I just went home and decided to do some research on the computer. I found three record stores within a ten mile radius of the park and decided to check them out. The first store was called Old Skool Records and they weren't hiring. I begged and pleaded but to no avail. The next store I checked out was called Di-Vinyl Records and again was denied employment, even after another beg and plead session. So I headed to the third and final record store on my short list. This one was called Gnarly Records, a name I loved when I first found it during my internet search.

When I walked in I was amazed. It was different than the

other two record stores, which were small one story places with not even half the records this place had. The main floor has rows and rows of records, thousands of them. The ceiling is like thirty feet high and there is a second story towards the back. The cashier counter is to the left by the front door. There is a guy behind the counter with long wavy hair and a goatee. He looks like a member of Soundgarden circa 1990. There are three people flipping through records on the main floor and no one that I could see upstairs. I walk up to the cashier counter and notice the name tag on the Soundgarden guy. It is in a plastic holder thing connected to a shoe string that is around his neck.

"Hey Rob. How's it going?"

He looks at me trying to figure out if he knows me. "Do I know you?"

"Nope, at least I don't think so."

"Then how do you know my name?"

Is this guy for real? "Um, your name tag." I point to it.

He looks down. "Oh yeah." He is not one bit embarrassed. He looks back at me. "Can I help you find something?"

"Well, I'm looking for something, but it's not a record." He gets a super confused look on his face.

"Well that's all we have here."

"Well I'm actually looking for a job Rob." I smile, a super fake one, actually a super cheesy fake one. He stares at me and then looks me up and down, fucking pig, but whatever I need this job.

"You ever work in a record store before?"

"No, but I love music and I'm a quick learner." I give him another super cheesy fake smile. He continues to look at me and then finally says something.

"What are your all-time top three records?"

"My all-time top three records?"

"That's what I said." I take a few seconds to think about the question.

"Um, number three would be *Never Mind the Bollocks, Here's the Sex Pistols.*"

He nods his head. "Okay, number two?"

"Number two would be…" I'm trying to think of records I actually like but that he might also like so he'll hire me. "I would have to say *Bleach* by Nirvana."

He nods his head again. "Okay, and number one?"

"Number one would have to be *In Rainbows* by Radiohead." I couldn't think of anything else because that record is actually my favorite record of all time and I could care less if he didn't like it. It's a brilliant record from the first track *15 step* to the last track *Videotape*, it's pure genius. He nods his head again and I'm feeling pretty good about this.

"Okay, those are all quality records." He continues to stare at me but we are interrupted by a customer wanting to check out.

"Why don't you take a walk around the store, let me help this guy, and then we can talk about it some more."

"Okay."

I turn around and walk down the first aisle I run into and start flipping through the R records, Rancid, REO Speedwagon, Richard Marx, etc. I look over and Rob is giving the customer his change. I walk further down the aisle and start flipping through the S records, The Smiths, Soundgarden, Stone Temple Pilots, etc. I hear the bell that is attached to the front door jingle and I look immediately. I see the door close and the customer walking past the front windows to the left down the sidewalk. I look over at Rob and he is staring at me. I assume he is contemplating if he wants to hire me and possibly sexually harass me in the future. I smile and he waves me over.

"So what's your name?"

"Zoe." He stares at me for several seconds.

"I need someone from five to close Wednesday through Saturday. If that's cool, then you're hired." I smile, a real one, a genuine smile and I forget to respond to Rob because I cannot believe it. "So, is that cool or not?"

I shake the smile thing from my mind and I answer him. "Yes, of course, that would be so cool Rob, thank you so much."

"Cool, so I will see you tomorrow at five. And just wear a band t-shirt like the one you have on and some jeans and I'll make you a name tag, okay?"

"Yeah, okay, I think I only have one other band t-shirt though."

"Just go to Hot Topic in the mall and get a couple more."

"Okay, yeah, cool, see ya tomorrow Rob." I start to walk towards the front door.

"Oh hey, how do I spell your name?"

"Z-O-E."

He writes it down on something. "Okay, cool, see ya."

"Later."

I push open the front door and the bell jingles and I walk down the sidewalk in the direction of my house with a smile on my face, a real one, and all I can think about is Ryan and if he will come in to my record store anytime soon.

When I get home I decide to call Dr. Wagner and tell him the good news. He is ecstatic and congratulates me on finding a job. He tells me to call him on Sunday to let him know how my first week at work went and I tell him I will.

I wake up Thursday morning at ten, shower, and get dressed. I find the only other band t-shirt I have, a Radiohead one I got at one of their concerts I went to a couple years ago. I decide to head to the mall and grab a couple of band t-shirts at Hot Topic. When I get to the mall I hit up the food court first and grab some Wetzel Pretzel bits with two sides of nacho cheese dip and a medium Diet Coke. I take a seat at a table and enjoy my little snack, which is actually very filling.

When I finish I toss my garbage in a trash can and then head to the closest mall directory to find out where the Hot Topic is. After searching for several seconds I find it, it is on the second floor on the other side of the mall. I walk down the ground floor of the mall, which I haven't been to in probably a year, and then take an escalator up to the second floor. When I reach the top of the escalator I see the Hot Topic ahead on the left.

I enter the store and am immediately attacked by some screamo music blasting out of the store speakers. The girl behind the counter looks like she is going to a Marilyn Manson concert after work. She is decked out in black everything, complete with black nail polish and lipstick and hoop piercings in her nose and lip. She smiles at me, a fake one I'm sure, and I smile back with a fake one of my own. The store walls on the entire left side are covered in band t-shirts and I peruse them looking for bands that I like, but that are also cool and hip or whatever. I decide to grab a Pink Floyd *Dark Side of the Moon* one, a *Never Mind the Bollocks Here's the Sex Pistols* one, and a Beatle's *Abbey Road* one. That will give me five shirts but I work four days a week so I decide to grab three more so I will have a different shirt over a two week period.

So I peruse the wall again and decide to grab a Nirvana *Nevermind* one, a Led Zeppelin *Houses of the Holy* one, and a Neil Diamond *The Jazz Singer* one. My dad loved Neil Diamond. He wanted to name me Caroline, but my mother didn't want to hear him sing that song to me the rest of her life so they settled on Zoe, which is a family name. It was my great grandmother's name on my mom's side. I head to the check-out counter and set the six shirts on the counter. The Goth girl behind the counter scans them.

"That will be a hundred and twenty-two sixty." My eyes get wide and I think to myself damn that's a bit much for six t-shirts but whatever. I give her my debit card and she slides it through the machine thingy. I punch in my pin number and it's approved. She throws the shirts into a black bag with Hot Topic written on it in red. Then she throws the receipt into the bag and hands it to me.

"Thank you." I say with another fake smile.

"Thank you. See ya next time." She says with a fake smile of her own.

I walk out of the store and head back down the mall, through the food court, and out the mall entrance doors. I get home a half hour later and decide to wash all my new shirts while I relax on the couch and watch a movie. I start my first day at Gnarly Records in four hours.

The dryer stops and buzzes just as the movie I was watching ends and I get up to take care of it. I grab the six shirts, take them to my closet, and hang them up. I decide to wear the Pink Floyd shirt and put it on. I don't start work for a couple of hours but I'm getting hungry again so I decide to go get some food and then head into work a little early. I'm sure I have to fill out some paperwork anyway. I head out the door twenty minutes later and stop by a local mom and pop sandwich shop for a half sandwich, a small salad, and a Diet Coke. This place makes a killer pastrami and chipotle coleslaw sandwich that is to die for and the Caesar salad is not too bad either.

As I eat I start to get a little nervous about working at the record store. I was stoked about getting the job but only because of the chance that Ryan would soon be walking through the doors. But what if he goes in before five? What if he goes in on Sunday or Monday or Tuesday? What if he doesn't even come to this record store? But he must, it's the best one of the three in this neighborhood. But what if he goes to one somewhere else that is really awesome? Oh well I guess I have to hope that one day he will come into the store when I'm there. I mean if it's meant to be then it will happen right? But in the meantime I have to talk to people I don't know and socialize with coworkers. Holy shit, what have I gotten myself into. I'm either going to get over all my shit real quick or I'm going to have a fucking meltdown and in the process lose my new job and my chance to get to know Ryan. I have to focus and battle through my issues and make this work.

I get to the record store fifteen minutes after four. Rob is behind the check-out counter and looks at me as the bell jingle jangles getting his attention.

"Zoe, you're early, nice."

"Hey Rob." I walk over to the counter. "I thought I would come in a little early and take care of any paperwork I needed to.

"Paperwork?"

"Yeah, tax forms, loyalty oaths, whatever." He looks at me with a confused look on his face. "Okay I was kidding about the loyalty oath, but the tax form, the W-2, you have to know about that?"

"Yeah, I've heard of that. Sherry takes care of all that stuff though, she's in the back." He points to the back of the store. "I will call her up." He grabs the phone receiver and presses a button on the phone base. His voice screeches throughout the store, which only has one customer at the moment. "Sherry please report to the front counter, Sherry please report to the front counter our new employee Zoe is here and is awaiting the filling out of her tax paperwork so she can pay her taxes like a nice little patriot." He hangs the phone up and smiles at me. At that same moment a woman, who I assume is Sherry, storms out of the back office.

"Rob are you fucking kidding me, you almost gave me a fucking heart attack." Rob starts laughing and I begin to chuckle a bit. Sherry finally arrives at the counter. She is older than me, probably in her early to mid-thirties. She has long jet black straight beautiful hair and green eyes. She is wearing a Credence Clearwater Revival t-shirt and blue jean.

"Sherry, Zoe, Zoe, Sherry." Rob introduces us. We shake hands and exchange fake smiles.

"It's nice to meet you."

"It's nice to meet you too Zoe. Let's head to the back and take care of the paperwork." She looks at Rob and points her right index finger at him. "And you…turn the volume down on that fucking intercom."

"Yessir massa, what eva ya say massa." He replies like a slave back on the plantation.

"Oh that's real funny Rob...and really fucking racist by the way." Sherry looks at me. "Let's go."

"Racist? No it's not...well maybe a little."

She glares at Rob then turns around and walks towards the back office, I follow. We enter the office and she takes a seat behind a small desk. I sit in the only other chair in the room, which is against the wall in front of the small desk. She grabs a couple papers out of one of the desk drawers and sets it down in front of me along with a pen. I fill out the W-2 and the employee information sheet and hand them back to her, along with the pen. She hands me my name tag, I put it around my neck and look at my name, which is spelled correctly.

"Welcome to Gnarly Records. I'm the owner by the way."

I look at her and she smiles at me. "Thank you for giving me the opportunity."

"No problem. Rob is a pain in the ass most of the time but he has always hired good people. I'm sure you will fit in just fine. And you look the part with the Pink Floyd shirt and the colored hair and nose piercing.

"I am who I am."

"That's good, we all should be who we are. I'm not a big fan of fake people."

"I couldn't agree more."

"Alright, follow me. I'll give you a quick rundown of how the store works. We stand and I follow Sherry as she exits the office and heads into the store. I cannot believe I have a new job, but it's a pretty cool job, at least I think it is.

"Okay, down here on the ground floor we have all of our rock slash pop records." She points to the left side and the center of the store. "And over here…" she points to the right side of the store, "…we have all of our jazz, blues, hip/hop, country, and soundtrack records." She then walks me back towards the office but takes the stairs up to the second floor, which is pretty small. "This is where the more valuable records are. If someone wants to check them out you have to take them up here and stay with them. If they want a record you take it down to the register and ring it up and get the money before they touch it." I nod my head to acknowledge that I understand.

We head back downstairs and she takes me to the front counter where Rob is. This of course is the front counter slash buy station slash listening station. If someone wants to listen to a record have them give it to you and you throw it gently on the turntable and play it over the store speakers. Do not, I repeat, do not let them do it. We have had issues in the past with people who have no idea how to handle vinyl scratching the shit out of records."

"Okay"

"If someone wants to sell us some records then call me on the intercom. I am the only one that buys records. If I'm not here tell them they need to come back when I am here, but I'm usually here so it shouldn't be a problem."

"Okay"

"Do you know how to work a cash register?"

"I have a little experience."

"Well you're going to shadow Rob for the rest of your shift today so just watch him and learn. He's a good trainer. And with that being said I now leave you in his capable hands. Take care of her Rob."

"Yes ma'am." She gives him a dirty look.

"You know how I feel about that ma'am shit."

He smiles. "Sorry boss won't happen again."

"Yes it will."

"Yeah probably."

I shadow Rob for the next five hours and he shows me everything I need to know and do and at the end of my shift I feel I have a pretty good handle on it. When the clock strikes ten Rob tells me to clock out and hit the road, which I do gladly. And as I head home I think to myself, damn, no sign of Ryan today, well maybe tomorrow or the next day or never.

Two days later, Saturday, I get a call from Dr. Wagner just before I'm about to head to work.

"Zoe, this is Dr. Wagner."

"Yeah I know. I thought I was supposed to call you tomorrow?"

"You are I just need your help with something, well this will actually help both of us."

"Sure what is it?"

"I need you to look for a record for me in your store and if you don't have it I need you to find it or order it or whatever. Can you do that for me?"

"Sure, what's the record?"

"It's called *Tyranny and Mutation* by Blue Oyster Cult."

"Is this for you Dr. Wagner?"

"No."

"I didn't think so."

"It's for Ryan." My eyes get wide and my heart begins to race.

"For Ryan. I don't get it."

"I just met with him at his house and he's not doing too well. He mentioned to me that he was looking for that record but he couldn't find it so I thought since you now work at a record store you might be able to get a hold of it. Then I thought I would tell him that I searched around and found it at your store. When do you work?"

"I work Wednesday through Saturday from five to ten."

"Okay, when you find it call me and I will call him and tell him that he can pick it up after five on any of those days."

"Okay."

"I figure this will help both of you out. It will cheer him up and give you an opportunity to interact with him instead of you just waiting on him to magically show up at your store when you're there, which could take a while."

"This is perfect Dr. Wagner. You're a genius."

"Well I don't know about that, but I do know how to help people Zoe."

"That you do Dr. Wagner, that you do."

We hang up and a smile forms on my face, a real one, a

genuine smile. Dr. Wagner is a genius and this plan is perfect. I can give him a record he has been looking for, which will cheer him up, and I get an opportunity to talk with him. Now all I have to do is find that record.

RYAN & ZOE

CHAPTER ELEVEN

My cellphone rings and I see that it's Dr. Wagner so I answer it.

"Hey doc, what's up?"

"Ryan, I have some good news."

"Oh yeah and what's that?"

"Well during my little house call a few days ago you were talking about a Blue Oyster Cult record called..." He tries to remember the name of the record.

"*Tyranny and Mutation* doc."

"Yes, that's it, *Tyranny and Mutation*. Well I made a few phone calls and I found it."

"No shit."

"No shit Ryan. I found it at a place called Gnarly Records. Do you know the place?"

"Yeah I've tried looking there before but with no luck."

"Well they must have gotten one in. I told them to hold it for you and they said you can come in tonight after five and pick it up."

"Wow, that's awesome doc, I really appreciate it."

"No problem Ryan, I thought it would cheer you up a bit."

"Yeah, it will definitely do that, thanks again doc."

"You're welcome Ryan. Enjoy it and I will see you tomorrow morning for our session."

"Yeah, see ya tomorrow doc."

I hang up, amazed that he did that for me. Dr. Wagner isn't such a stuffy douchebag after all. I look at the time on my cellphone and its only noon. "What the hell am I going to do for five hours?" I say out loud to myself. I contemplate just lying in bed but decide that I'm too amped for that and I decide to get up and walk around the neighborhood for a little while. I can't wait to listen to that record later tonight, it is so much better on vinyl than on my IPod.

When I get back from my walk it is still only two o'clock so I decide to listen to some records. I'm feeling like some old school punk music so I grab The Ramones self-titled debut record and gently lay the needle down on the first track, *Blitzkrieg Bop*. I can't help but sing along, out loud, with Joey.

"They're forming in a straight line. They're going through a tight wind. The kids are losing their minds. The Blitzkrieg

Bop... " After listening to the A-side I decide to listen to something else. I grab something totally different, a Hall and Oates record titled *H2O* and gently drop the needle down on the first track, *Maneater*. I have loved this song since the first time I heard it, many years ago. Again, I have to sing out loud.

"...Oh-oh, here she comes. Watch out boy she'll chew you up. Oh-oh, here she comes. She's a maneater..."

After listening to that A-side I again switch records and repeat this for the next three hours. I listen to everything from Jimi Hendrix to John Coltrane to Neil Diamond to Radiohead. I am immersed in the raw beautiful sound that is vinyl. Cassette tapes and compact discs and fucking Mp3s have destroyed music. Sure its cleaner, but only pop music is okay when it's cleaned up like that. Rock music and jazz and blues, should only be listened to on vinyl. When it's not you lose the soul of the song, you miss parts of it that are filtered out on CDs and Mp3s. Those genres of music are supposed to be raw and edgy and scratchy, it makes them more alive and in turn makes the listener more alive.

I fucking love vinyl records and I'm saddened by this younger generation and my generation who are missing out on it. And the future generations who will also miss out on it because they aren't exposed to it like I was as a kid. One of the best parts of my childhood was when my dad and I would sit around and just listen to vinyl record after vinyl record and I was blown away. I was fucking five years old and I was getting inundated with these classic records and it changed my life.

Fifteen minutes before five I get up and head to the record store to finally grab the Blue Oyster Cult record that I've been looking for, for years. I could have bought it online but there is no fun in that; the fact that Dr. Wagner found it and I didn't find it myself kind of sucks, but I'll take it. The air has a bit of a chill tonight as I walk down the street, which is busy with cars as people head home from work. All I hear is car engines and the occasional honking of a car horn.

I fucking hate the sound of car horns. My father used to honk at everything when he drove, other cars, people, animals, etc. He honked so much the front of his steering wheel where the horn is was worn out. He would even honk at nothing sometimes, like when he got to the end of an alley he would honk just in case someone flying down the sidewalk on a bike or a skateboard wouldn't run into the side of his car, which is okay I guess. The horn is supposed to be used as a warning device, but most people use it to annoy everyone else. I honestly believe that if cars didn't have horns ninety percent of all incidents of road rage would have never happened.

The sun begins to penetrate the horizon to my left as I continue through the neighborhood towards the record store. As I approach the coffee shop where Sherrie and I spent many an afternoon sipping cappuccinos and eating pastries, I feel a pain in my chest. Memories shoot into my head like a shotgun blast and I stop in front of the café's floor to ceiling windows and peer inside. It is practically empty except for the twenty-something female barista behind the counter who is reading a book and a lone guy wearing dark rimmed glasses in the corner working on his laptop, a Mac of course, fucking hipster. I stand there long enough for the barista to notice and she lowers her book and stares at me. I stare back at her and smile. She doesn't smile back and goes back to her book, which is probably some shitty old novel that she's required to read for some pointless college course. I shake the barrage of memories from my head, literally, and continue my walk to the record store, which I finally arrive at ten minutes after five.

I attempt to push open the door but to no avail. Then I notice the pull sticker just above the handle and I instantly feel like an idiot. I regroup and pull the door open. A bell above the door jingles to announce to the entire store that I have arrived, but you can't really hear it because the speakers are blasting with some artsy-fartsy folk music, you know, the kind with mandolins and sitars and shit. I notice a guy behind the front counter and I head that way.

"Hey I'm here to pick up a record." I yell just in case he can't hear me over the insane ukulele solo that is melting the speakers. Yes, that was sarcasm.

"What record?" He yells back.

"Blue Oyster Cult. *Tyranny and Mutation.*" He looks at me confused.

"We have that?"

"I don't know. A friend of mine called and had someone hold it for me."

"Okay, let me check." He grabs the phone receiver from its base and yells into it. "Zoe you're needed at the front counter, please pull your pants up, flush, and come to the front counter. Oh, and don't forget to wash your hands." He sets the receiver down and smiles at me.

"Real funny Rob." I turn my head and I see the girl from Dr. Wagner's office quickly walking through the store towards us. She makes eye contact with me and smiles.

"Ryan, right?" she says as I stand there speechless, staring at her hair, which now has streaks of blue and green in it. "You're name is Ryan isn't it?" I break out of my trance.

"Yeah, how do you know my name?" I ask even though I already know the answer.

"Our mutual friend told me." She obviously doesn't want Rob here to know that she sees a shrink.

"Oh, so that's how he found the record." She nods. "So where is it?"

"It's right back here." She walks passed me and I can smell her perfume again just like I did in Dr. Wagner's waiting room. She goes behind the front counter, reaches down underneath the cash register, and comes back up with the record in her hand. She rings it up on the register. "That'll be twenty seven thirty five." I hand her the cash and she hands me the record and then the receipt.

"Thanks." I say as I start to turn to leave.

"That's it?" She says and I turn back toward her.

"What?" I say even though I heard her.

"Nothing. Nevermind." She takes a deep breath and exhales loud enough that I can hear it over the music in the store. I have no idea what she wants from me so I say the first thing that enters my head.

"Do you want to listen to it?" I raise the record I just purchased.

"Sure, hand it over and I'll put it on." She shoots her arm towards me. I start to raise my arm to hand it to her but for some unknown reason I stop and then lower my arm. "What's wrong?"

"Nothing, I just really wanted to listen to it at home."

"Oh." She has a look of sadness and confusion on her face.

"I just really love the sound my player puts out and I just wanted to lay on my bed and zone out to it." Wow, that was a little too much information.

"Oh, okay."

We stare at each other and I don't know what to do or say. It is one of those awkward moments that everyone has about a thousand times during their life. So I just blurt something out to break the awkwardness of the scene.

"Do you want to come over and listen to it with me?" For some unknown reason that came out of my mouth and I am as shocked by it as she apparently is.

"Really?" She says with a smile. There is no way I can back out of this one.

"Sure, why not?" Well maybe because you're a fucking emotional basket case right now, I say in my head.

"Okay, yeah, but I don't get off until ten."

"That's fine you can come over then. I stay up pretty late so…"

"Okay, where do you live?" I think about giving her my address but it's my brother's place and I honestly don't remember it.

"Um, why don't I just come back here at ten and we can walk there or take the bus, unless you have a car."

"I don't drive so no car, but yeah we can walk."

"Okay, well see ya at ten then."

"Okay, see ya." I turn and walk out of the store and as the sound of the doorbell jingles in my head I think to myself, what the hell just happened there?

When I get back to the house Mitch is on the couch watching TV and eating something.

"Hey bro, what ya got there?"

"A record."

"Cool, which one?"

"It's just some Blue Oyster Cult record I've been looking for." I start to head toward my room.

"Hey, there's some spaghetti on the stove if you're hungry."

"Yeah okay, thanks."

I continue to my room, toss the record on my bed, and then head to the kitchen. I grab a bowl out of the cabinet, fill it with spaghetti, and then head to the living room to join my brother. I take a seat on the couch next to him and start eating. He's watching some documentary about some dolphin slaughter in Japan.

"So what's been up with you lately?" he says.

"What do you mean?" I swirl some spaghetti around my fork and take a bite.

"I don't know. It's been awhile since we've talked. I was just curious what you've been up to."

"Not much, same old stuff."

"How's the therapy going?"

"I really don't want to talk about that."

"Okay." He takes his final bite of spaghetti and sets his plate down on the coffee table.

"Oh, hey, this chick is gonna come over later if that's cool?" He has a shocked look on his face, like he just found out his girlfriend is pregnant.

"No shit."

"Yeah, but it's no big deal she's just a friend. Well not even really a friend just someone I met at the record store. She sold me that record I had."

"That's great bro. Is she cute?"

"It's not like that Mitch, you know I'm emotionally crippled right now. She just wanted to hear the record so I invited her over. I regretted it the moment I said it, but I couldn't take it back."

"Well, whatever it is, it's good that you're making friends and being more social. It's progress bro."

"Jesus, you sound like my fucking shrink."

I finish up my bowl of spaghetti, get up, grab Mitch's
empty plate and fork and take them to the kitchen. I rinse
everything off and load them into the dishwasher. I head to my
room without saying another word to my brother. I grab the
record off of the bed and then lay down on the bed. The record
is used and doesn't have any plastic around it. I examine the
cover and then flip it over and check out the track list on the
back. I carefully remove the record and examine it for any
scratches, which I usually do before I buy a record but I was
distracted by Zoe and forgot to.

The record is in decent shape there are only a couple of
small surface scratches, nothing that will affect the sound. I sit
up, stand up, and head to my record player. I lift the lid and
gently lay the record on the turntable. I turn it on, gently set
the needle on track four, *7 Screaming Diz-Busters*, close the
top, and then lie back down on the bed. I smile and start
singing out loud as the first verse begins. *"They held their
heads with laughs of pain. They learned from men who'd just
refrain. From glancing at a mirror's face. Seven screaming
diz-busters who lurked by a rose. Had iron for a bloodstream
and ice behind their eyes."* When the song ends I close my
eyes and envision Shellie lying next to me, but when I open
my eyes and look, it is just the record sleeve lying there. I
close my eyes again and for some strange reason I see Zoe
lying next to me, smiling.

I must have fallen asleep because I jolt myself awake and
grab my phone to check the time in a panic thinking that it's

past ten and that I have stood up Zoe, but it's only nine and I take a deep breath and try to calm the beating in my chest. I lie in bed for thirty more minutes, zoned out, staring at the ceiling, thinking about nothing in particular. Then I get up and head out the front door. I get to the record store five minutes before close and flip through some records waiting for Zoe. She comes out from the back smiling. Her hair is up in a ponytail and she is wearing a Beatles t-shirt, jeans, and a pair of black low top Chuck Taylors. All of which I didn't notice earlier.

"You're here?" She says somewhat surprised.

"What? Did you think I wouldn't show?"

"It crossed my mind."

"You owe me five bucks." Rob yells toward Zoe from behind the front counter as he counts up the cash register.

"It looks like it." She yells back. I look at her slightly confused and she looks at me and smiles. "Rob said you'd show."

"And you bet him five bucks that I wouldn't?"

She shrugs her shoulders. "It was a win-win bet."

"Yeah, I guess so. You ready?"

"Yep, let's go." I turn and we walk towards the front doors. "How far is it anyways?"

"It's a twenty, twenty-five minute walk. I say as we exit the store, the bell jingling.

"Okay, cool."

We walk in silence for a few minutes before Zoe starts up a

conversation.

"So why are you seeing Dr. Wagner?" I look at her like are you really asking me that question and she senses that she probably shouldn't have started with that question.

"I don't really want to get into that right now."

"Okay, sorry."

"It's okay."

"So are you from here?" She asks.

"Yep, born and raised. You?"

"We moved here when I was nine. My dad was offered a promotion at work. Relocating was part of the deal. It was more money and we really didn't have any ties to where we were so he took it."

"Where did you guys move from?"

"Minneapolis."

"Wow that's a ways away."

"Yep. His company paid for movers so we just basically got in the car and headed west."

"You like Seattle?" I ask.

"I love it. How about you?

"Well, it's all I know. I haven't lived anywhere else. I could do without all the rain, but the summers are awesome."

"Yes they are. I don't mind the rain, it's a lot better than all the snow we got in Minneapolis. I was just a kid but I remember how cold the winters were, it was brutal."

"Yeah I bet. We've gotten snow here but nothing like there I'm sure."

"Not even close." We come to the coffee shop I have passed now for the fourth time today, the one Shellie and I used to go to.

"You want to grab a coffee." She says.

"Not from there."

"Okay." I can tell by the way she said it that I should explain but I really don't want to so I make up a little white lie.

"There's another place down the street that has better coffee, we can stop in there."

"Okay, cool."

We reach the other coffee place, order two large lattes to go, and continue on towards my place, or I should say my brother's place.

"Oh and just so you don't freak out, I live with my brother right now, so we might see him if he's still up."

"Oh, okay."

We walk the next few minutes in silence, drinking our lattes. It's a bit chilly out tonight and the coffee is definitely helping us keep warm.

"So how long have you been working at the record store?"

"This is my second week."

"Oh really, that's all?"

"Yeah, it was actually Dr. Wagner's idea."

"Really?"

"Yeah, well getting a job was his idea, the record store is just what I found."

"Good old Dr. Wagner and his ideas."

"It's all part of the process." She says in her best Dr. Wagner voice, which makes me laugh.

"He's an alright guy." I say as I look up and notice the moon, which is barely visible through the clouds.

"Yeah, he's pretty cool, except for those hideous socks he wears."

"What? You don't like his socks?"

"Not at all."

"Wow, I think they're awesome."

"Well we're just going to have to agree to disagree."

We get to the house and I unlock the door. My brother is nowhere to be seen and I assume he is already in bed. I put my right index finger to my lips letting Zoe know to be quiet and she acknowledges that she understands by nodding and mouthing a silent okay. We quietly make our way to my room which is on the opposite side of the house from my brother's room. We enter and Zoe sits down on the bed. I set what's left of my coffee on the night stand and then throw my wallet and cellphone next to it.

"So are we gonna listen to this record or is it too late?"

"No it's fine, we just have to keep the volume down a bit."

"Cool."

"The sleeve is right there if you want to check it out." I point to it. It's behind her on the bed where I left it earlier. She reaches back, grabs it, and checks it out. The record is still on the turntable so I lift the lid, turn it on, and gently lay the needle down on the first track, The Red and The Black. As the song kicks into the first verse Zoe notices my record collection.

"That is quite a record collection ya got there."

"Yeah, it's not too bad."

"How many records do you have?

"Oh about three hundred. It's a small collection but everything in there is great. It's about quality, not quantity." She sets the *Tyranny and Mutation* sleeve back down on the bed, gets off the bed, and takes a seat on the floor in front of my collection.

"Can a look through them?"

"Of course, help yourself." She starts thumbing through them. "If you see something you want to listen to just pull it out and I will throw it on."

"Okay." She continues to thumb through records as I lie down on the bed.

"So you must be into vinyl since you work at a record store huh?"

"Too be completely honest, when I went into the store to see if they were hiring last week that was the first time I had actually been in a vinyl record store."

"You're kidding?"

"Nope and to be even more honest, it was also the first time I had heard music from a vinyl record."

My jaw drops as she looks at me. "That's insane."

"Maybe, but I'm not that old, hell I don't remember ever

listen to music on a cassette tape now that I think about it."

"How old are you by the way? I mean if you don't mind me asking?"

"I'm almost twenty-five. How old are you?"

"Guess."

"Oh, we're playing games now are we?"

"I always ask people to guess, it's a habit. You don't have to if you don't want to."

"No, I'll give it a shot." She looks intensely at my face, studying it. "I'm gonna say you are...twenty-nine."

"Wow, that's close. I will actually be twenty-nine in four months."

"It's the beard, it makes you look older. If you were clean shaven I would have said twenty-eight." She goes back to thumbing through the records.

"Yeah, sure you would have." She pulls a record out, examines the front and back covers, and extends it towards me.

"I wanna hear this one." I notice the cover immediately and I take it from her. It's Led Zeppelin's *Houses of the Holy*.

"Okay, cool. I love this record. It's actually my favorite Zeppelin record." I jump off the bed and set the record on the bed. "You want a quick lesson on how to properly handle a vinyl record? Oh wait, you work at a record store."

"Actually, I have yet to be trained in the fine art of laying down vinyl." I can't tell if she's telling the truth or bullshitting me, but I proceed with the lesson anyway.

"Okay, stand up." She stands up. I open the clear plastic lid. "Okay, first things first, gently lift the needle off of the record, straight up so you don't scratch it, and then set it gently on its rest. Then turn it off. Some people will turn it off first and then remove the needle once it stops, but that's no fun. Then remove the record by lifting it straight up off of the turntable with your hands on the outside edges like this. You don't want to touch the playing surface because the oils from your fingers will screw up the grooves."

I notice she is listening intently, which is awesome, and I continue on. "Then, if your hands are big enough, which mine are, you hook your thumb on the edge like this and then rest your fingers on the center part of the record where there are no grooves like this." She is still totally into it and I'm not sure if she is really interested or if she is just being nice. "Am I being to descriptive here?"

"Not at all, I love it. Your passion for it is intoxicating."

"Really?"

"Yeah, go on."

"Okay, well next you grab the sleeve." I walk over to the bed and grab it. "Now I call this whole thing the sleeve, but the sleeve is actually this thin protective thing in the cover." I open the cover with one hand and show her the sleeve inside. "Now this is where I don't get too anal about it. Most people will take the sleeve out, put the record in it and then slide the sleeve into the cover so that you can't see the record, which protects it better. I just leave the sleeve in the cover and just slide it in like this. See how you can see the edge of the record?"

"Yeah."

"Well, people would give me shit for that but whatever, I love vinyl, but I'm not psycho about it." I bend down and add the record to my collection. "Oh, and there is no rhyme or reason to my organization. After I listen to a record I just put it where ever.

"No alphabetical order?"

"Nope, that's too conformist, I just like flipping through them and when I come across something I want to listen to I listen to it."

"Well what if you want to listen to a specific record?"

"Then I flip through them until I find it, but to be honest I will usually play something else and forget about what I was looking for." I smile and she smiles back.

"So is that it?"

"Yeah, well to put a record on you just do exactly what I just did but in reverse."

"Cool. Thanks for the lesson." There was not one drop of sarcasm in her statement.

"You are welcome. Now let's get this Zeppelin spinnin'." I put the Zeppelin record on the turntable and gently drop the needle on track one, which is *The Song Remains the Same*. I close the lid and lie back down on the bed.

"Mind if I join you?"

I wasn't expecting her to say that and it through me off a

bit. "Um, yeah, sure."

She walks over to the other side of the bed and lies down next to me. I think back to earlier today when I had imagined this happening in my head, but in no way did I think it would actually happen. I begin to freak out a little bit. "I just want to be friends okay?" I blurt out quickly as I stare at the ceiling.

"I'm just lying next to you Ryan, I'm not trying to make out with you."

"I know, I'm just sayin." I'm still staring at the ceiling. I'm afraid that if I look at her my body will tell my mind to piss off and I can't have that.

"Statement dually noted." She says.

We lie there in silence as track two, *The Rain Song*, starts. When the third track, *Over the Hills and Far Away*, begins I break the silence, so to speak.

"This is my favorite Zeppelin song."

"It's a good one."

"This was my dad's favorite band. He fucking loved these guys."

"Was?"

"Yeah, the cancer got him three years ago."

"I'm sorry."

"Yeah, it's shitty, but what are ya gonna do? I've learned that you can't do anything about the things you don't have any control over, just the things you do. If that makes any sense?"

"Yeah, it makes a lot of sense." I hear her sniffle and I finally look over at her and she is staring at the ceiling and I can see a tear slide down her left cheek.

"You okay?"

She wipes the tears from her eyes. "Yeah, I'm fine." She looks at me and smiles, just like my vision earlier, and I smile back. "What about your mother?"

"She couldn't handle staying here so she went to Phoenix to take care of my grandmother." The A-side of the record ends and we sit in silence for a couple minutes. "So what about your parents?" Zoe begins to cry more and I suddenly realize why she has been seeing Dr. Wagner. "I'm sorry."

"I'm not ready to talk about it."

"Understood."

"I should get going."

"Okay." I get up from the bed and head to the bathroom where I grab some toilet paper and then return to the room. She is standing up now at the foot of the bed. I extend my arm and offer her the toilet paper.

"Sorry, I don't have any regular tissue." She takes the toilet paper and chuckles a little.

"That's okay, thank you." She wipes the tears from her face and eyes and then blows her nose. We are standing there, face to face, and I have no idea what to say so I do the first thing that comes to my mind and I give her a hug. She hugs me back and cries some more into my shoulder. After what feels like forever we release and she wipes away the tears once again.

"How are you getting home? Do you want me to walk with

you?"

"No you don't have to, I kinda want to be alone for a bit."

"Okay. Can I at least walk you to the sidewalk?"

She smiles and wipes her nose. "I would like that."

I open my bedroom door and walk her through the house, out the front door, and to the sidewalk. It is a bit chilly and Zoe is visibly cold.

"Wait here, I'll be back in a sec." I say.

"Okay."

I run into the house and then run back out to her. "Here take this." I hand her my University of Washington hoodie and she takes it.

"Are you sure?"

"Yeah, it's pretty chilly out and I would feel bad if you died of pneumonia on the walk home."

She chuckles and smiles. "Thank you."

I smile back at her. "You are very welcome. And thanks for coming over, it was nice to have someone to listen to records with and to talk to."

"It was very nice, thanks for having me."

With that said we hug again and she turns and walks down the street. I watch her until she turns the corner and disappears. I head back inside and jump into my warm bed. I lie there as thoughts explode in head like the grand finale of a fourth of July fireworks show and I slowly fade away into the dream world that awaits me.

CHAPTER TWELVE

Someone pounding on my bedroom door wakes me up but I don't move. The pounding continues and gets louder each time.

"Ryan, wake up its three in the afternoon."

It's my brother but I ignore him, but he's a persistent bastard and continues to bang on the door like a madman.

"What do you want?" I yell, half asleep.

"Dr. Wagner called. He's called you like five times. You need to call him back."

I don't hear a word he says. "Just come in and talk to me." I say, still half asleep.

Mitch opens my bedroom door. "Dr. Wagner wants you to

call him."

"Okay, shit. I will call him when I get up." I pull the covers over my head.

"It's three in the afternoon Ryan, wake the fuck up."

"Alright man, shit, give me a second."

"Hey how did it go with that chick last night by the way?" I throw the covers off of me and look at him. "It went okay."

"Did you make out with her?"

I glare at him. "I told you, we're just friends, don't be a dick."

"Alright, alright geez, relax. Just call the doc back as soon as possible okay?"

"Alright." I yell back. He closes the door. "Hey Mitch?"

He opens it back up. "Yeah."

"Do you think you can take me and Zoe to Twin Fall Saturday morning?"

"Yeah, sure bro, I can do that."

"Cool man, thanks."

"Anytime. I love you."

I take a deep breath and groan as I exhale. "I love you too."

He closes the door again and I grab my phone. Mitch was right, Dr. Wagner called me five times and left two voicemails. I decide to just call him without listening to the voicemails.

"Hello." Dr. Wagner answers.

"Dr. Wagner, what's the emergency?"

"No emergency, I just want to see how thing were going."

"Things are not too bad."

"That's good to hear, did you get the record I had held for you?"

"I did, thanks again."

"You're welcome. And did you get a chance to talk to Zoe?"

"I did." I am a bit hesitant to give him the full details but decide that it doesn't matter. "She actually came over last night and listened to records with me."

"Really?" He seemed a tad shocked.

"Yeah, she's actually not the complete bitch that I thought she was."

"She's a sweetheart Ryan. You just have to get passed her tough exterior."

"Yeah she's pretty cool. I'm actually going to ask her if she wants to go for a little hike this Saturday."

"That's great Ryan, she will love that I'm sure." There is a short silence and all I can hear is Dr. Wagner breathing. "Well, anyway, I'm glad you are doing well and I will see you next week."

"Okay doc, talk to ya later." I hit the end call button on my cellphone and toss it back onto the night stand. I stretch out my entire body and then get out of bed. I shower, get dressed, and then throw on a record, The White Stripe's *Elephant*. I lie in bed until the A-side of the record ends and then I get up, stretch, and then head out the front door. I stop at a local burger joint and grab a burger, fries, and a vanilla shake. I look at my cellphone to check the time; its five minutes until five. I finish up my late lunch and then make my way to Zoe's record store. The jingle of the front door bell announces my presence. I see Zoe right away. She is checking someone out at the front counter register. She turns and sees me as I approach the counter and she smiles. I smile back. She finishes up with her customer and then steps out from behind the counter.

"Hey." She says with a huge smile.

"Hey."

"You come to see me or checkout the records?" Her hair is once again in a ponytail but no longer has colored streaks in it, it is completely white blond.

"You took the color out of your hair."

"I did, you noticed, that's very observant of you."

"I try."

"I wanna color all of it but I haven't decided if I want it pink, blue, or orange. What do you think?"

"I would say pink."

"I will take that under advisement. You didn't answer my question by the way?

"What question?"

"Are you here to see me or check out records?"

"Well, I'm actually here to ask you a question."

"Oh yeah, what's that?"

"Well, I wanted to hike the Twin Falls Trail Saturday and I thought you might want to go with me." She has an, are you serious look on her face.

"Are you asking me on a date?"

I shake my head. "Not at all, just two friends walking through the woods, that's all."

She doesn't seem to like my answer. "Okay."

"Is that an okay yes you'll go?"

She nods her head. "Yes Ryan, I would love to walk through the woods with you."

"Cool. My brother and I will pick you up at your place at nine Saturday morning."

"Your brother is going with us?"

"No. he's just taking us since neither one of us drives."

"Oh, okay."

A customer approaches the front counter. "I have to go. I'll see you Saturday?"

"Yep, see you Saturday."

I watch her walk behind the counter and proceed to help the customer. She turns and looks at me and smiles. I smile back and then turn and leave the store. When I get home I lie in bed and listen to records for the rest of the night. As I lay there, for some unknown reason, all I can think about is seeing Zoe on Saturday.

Saturday morning comes quicker than I had expected and I awake to the sound of the alarm on my cellphone. I haven't been up this early in a long time if you don't count the many a nights I never got to sleep. I get out of bed and head to the bathroom. I toss my medications into my mouth and wash them down with sink water using my cupped hand. I turn on the shower and remove my boxer shorts. I hop in the shower and the hot water awakens my senses like a strong cup of coffee and a cigarette. I stand under the shower head and let the water attack the top of my head as it runs down my body and finally reaches the drain. After about twenty minutes I turn the water off and towel off. I get dressed and head to the kitchen where Mitch is grinding coffee beans for a pot of coffee.

"Hey little brother, ready for your big date?"

I glare at him. "It's not a date, we're just friends."

He chuckles. "Yeah, sure." He says like he doesn't believe me.

"Just make the coffee."

"Yes sir boss." He says like the giant Black guy from *The Green Mile*. "So where does this Zoe chick live?"

I think for a minute and I realize that I never asked her for her address. "Shit."

"You never got her address did you?"

"I totally forgot."

"Do you at least have her number?"

I realize that I never got that either. "Shit" I say a little louder this time.

"Um, bro how the hell are we supposed to pick her up if we don't know where she lives?" I scratch the top of my head with my right hand and then slide it down my face.

"That's a great question and I have no idea."

"Hey, call Dr. Wagner and see if he will give you her address or number."

I look at him like I can't believe he actually said something intelligent. "That might work. Let me give him a call." I run to my room, grab my cellphone, and hit the call button after I find him in my contacts.

"Ryan, what's wrong? Are you okay?" The doc sounds worried about me.

"I'm fine doc I just need a favor."

"What is it?"

"My brother and I are supposed to pick up Zoe and I never got her address or her phone number. Is there any chance I can get it from you?"

"I can't do it Ryan. That would be a violation of doctor, patient confidentiality, you know that."

"Damn. Well what am I gonna do doc? I just can't not show up."

"Calm down. I will just call her and give her your number if that's okay with you?"

"That's not a violation?"

"Not if you say it's okay."

"Yeah, its fine doc, go ahead, and thank you, you're a lifesaver."

"Anytime Ryan you know that."

"Okay, talk to you later doc."

"Sure thing."

I hit the end call button on my cellphone and head back to the kitchen. The smell of fresh brewed coffee and cooking bacon fills the room, which might just be the best smell in the history of humanity.

"He couldn't give me her number but he is going to call her and give her mine."

He has a confused look on his face. "What? Why?"

"It's a confidentiality thing."

"Oh, gotcha. You want some bacon?"

"Did you really just ask me that question? Of course I want some bacon."

I walk over to the cabinet above the coffee maker and grab a mug. I grab the carafe from the coffee maker and pour it into the mug, leaving room for some French vanilla creamer, which I grab from the refrigerator. We stand in the kitchen eating bacon and drinking coffee when my cellphone beeps.

I look at it and there is a new text message. I open it and it's an address. I text her back *thank u see u at 9*. A few seconds later she text's me back *k* :).

"That was Zoe. Thank God."

"Got the address?" My brother asks with a mouth full of bacon.

"Yep." I take a bite of a strip of bacon eating half of it and then I wash it down with a big gulp of coffee.

We leave the house twenty minutes later in my brother's dark green 1999 Subaru Forester, which is basically just a station wagon for yuppies and hipsters and is a total Seattle cliché. But it's a good solid vehicle and you can camp in it which is one of the reasons it is so popular up here. We get to Zoe's place at nine on the dot. Her house is nice. It's your typical one story house with an underneath garage, Swiss looking shutters, and dark wood roof shingles. My brother honks the horn and several seconds later Zoe exits her house and skips down the walkway to the car. She is wearing a white North Face pullover, another Seattle cliché, jeans, and a beanie hat that looks like a panda bear. Her hair is down and I can see that she went with pink for the new color. She opens the back door and climbs in.

"Hey guys."

"Hey Zoe." We both say at the same time.

"Mitch this is Zoe, Zoe this is my big brother Mitch.

"It's nice to meet you Zoe."

"It's nice to me you too Mitch."

My brother drives off and we spend the next thirty minutes listening to Jack Johnson, which is all my brother listens to, and chatting about the weather and how badass my brother's Forester is. Well, Zoe was mostly chatting about that, but I couldn't argue with her, I love this damn wagon.

We pull into the trailhead and park between two other Subaru's, another Forester and an Outback. There are about five other cars parked in the lot, which is common on a Saturday morning, even though it is a little chilly. Zoe and I get out, but my brother stays in the car.

"He's not coming with us?"

"Nah, he has some reading to do."

"Oh, okay." She smiles and I smile back.

"See you in an hour or so Mitchy."

He looks up from his book. "You kids have fun. Don't do anything I wouldn't do?"

"Yeah, yeah."

We head down the trail, which at first hugs the river bank.

"Your brother's a nice guy."

"Yeah, he's pretty cool."

"You guys seem like you have a good relationship."

"Yeah, I mean we have moments where we want to kill each other but what siblings don't right?"

"True."

"Do you have any brothers or sister?" She doesn't respond for several seconds.

"I don't want to talk about that if that's okay?" I can see her eyes begin to well up with tears but she fights them off and they never fall.

"Yeah, sorry."

"No, I'm sorry. I'll tell you about my family someday Ryan, just not today."

"Okay."

I see a little cove just passed some trees about twenty-five yards away and suggest that we take a look at it. Zoe agrees and we leave the trail and make our way through the trees to the cove. The river is a good sized one, about forty feet wide where we are. There are black and grey rocks and boulders sticking out of the ice cold water throughout the river and tall green trees surround it, protecting it, like soldiers standing guard. The clouds are low this morning and you can see the sun trying to pierce its rays through them but to no avail. I look down, squat down, and grab a handful of thin rocks. I stand back up and extend my open, rock-filled hand towards Zoe. She looks at me like what am I supposed to do with these?

"For skipping." She lifts her head as to say oh okay I get it now. She takes a few and then attempts to skip one across the river but it only skips once, which is not really a skip but more like a plop. "Have you ever done this before?"

"Maybe."

"Maybe? Oh my God, please don't tell me that you've never skipped rocks before."

"Okay, so I've never skipped rocks before, are you happy." She says in a playful tone.

"No, I'm not happy. This is a travesty and it must be corrected. Today, right now, you will learn to skip a rock." She laughs and her smile stops me in my tracks and my brain shuts down. I can't formulate a single word. "So are you gonna show me or what?"

I snap out of it. "Yeah, yeah, of course. Now the first thing you need to do, besides finding the flattest rocks, is you need to hold the rock correctly. Now place your index finger across the edge of the rock like this and then hold it with your thumb and middle finger like this." I demonstrate. "Then when you throw it you get your arm as low as possible and then flick your wrist at the end. I demonstrate. It should skip at least five times. That is what I go for at least. The more skips the better.

Mitch and I used to have contests to see who could get the most skips, we were super competitive, and still are. I guarantee you if he was here we would be competing."

I skip a rock almost all the way across the river on my first attempt and Zoe looks thoroughly impressed, but probably not. "Okay let's see if you're a good listener. Go ahead a give it a shot."

She grabs a rock from her left hand, checks her grip, winds up, and lets it go. It skips four times, almost halfway across the river and she jumps up and down. "I did it, I did it." She continues to jump up and down and then jumps into my arms and gives me a hug.

I am taken back, not expecting her to do that. She loosens her embrace and looks into my eyes. We stare at each other for several seconds and I can sense that she wants to kiss me but wants me to make the first move, which I don't. My body and my heart and my brain are engaged in a full on assault against one another, but the brain prevails and I break the silence and the tension. "That was impressive. We should skip the rest of these and then get back on the trail."

"Okay."

I can tell she is slightly dejected and I try to think of something to say, a compliment. "I love your panda beanie by the way." I say with a smile.

"Thanks. It's my favorite article of clothing." She smiles back.

We finish skipping our rocks and then head back to the

trail. We take the trail about a mile further and reach one of the waterfalls that are along the trail. It is the largest one, about a hundred feet high. The white water is pouring over the falls and is making that unique sound that only a waterfall can make. It is peaceful and we just stand there and watch it and listen to nature's symphony. Zoe rests her head on my left shoulder and for some unknown reason I put my left arm around her and my heart explodes. I am quietly hyperventilating inside, but I don't want this moment to end so I battle through it. My brain, body, and heart are going at it again, but this time there is no winner.

After several minutes we head back down the trail towards the car and Mitch. Our hands brush each other's as we walk, but I am reluctant to go ahead and hold hers.

"So what do you do? For work?" She asks me.

"Well, nothing at the moment. I'm on medical leave, but before that I was a part-time substitute teacher. I guess I still am, but I put it on hold for the time being. What about you?"

"I work at a record store, duh."

"I mean before the record store."

"Well, before the record store, nothing, but before…" She pauses. "…but before my current issues, I did pedicures and manicures at this salon owned by a friend of mine."

"That's cool, are you going to get back into that?

"I don't know. I thought about finishing school but I haven't decided yet."

"School huh? What were you studying?"

"I was studying business. I wanted to open up my own nail place, but I don't know if I want to do that anymore."

"What are you thinking about doing instead?"

"I have no idea. Maybe I'll just stay at the records store. " We continue walking and pass the place where we skipped rocks. "So what did you teach?"

"Whatever they told me to. That's the life of a substitute, you just go in and they tell you what class you'll be covering that day. It could be science or math or English or history or even art or some other elective."

"Do you like it?"

"It's okay. It's easy money, I just go in and do whatever the teacher left for me and then I leave."

"How much do you make doing that? If you don't mind me asking."

"No, it's fine. I make between eighty and a hundred a day depending on the district. It's not great money but it pays the bills. And I don't have a ton of bills so I manage to survive okay."

We reach the trailhead and make our way back to the car. Mitch is now in the back taking a nap. I bang on the back window. "Mitchy, wake up."

He jumps up and hits his head on the roof of the car. "Jesus Ryan, are you trying to give me a fucking heart attack?"

"Maybe. Let's go, I'm hungry." Mitch jumps out of the back and gets in the driver's seat. I tell Zoe to take the front seat.

"Do you mind if I sit in the back with you?" She says with a head tilt and a smile.

"Sure." We climb in the back seat and Mitch looks at us through the rear view mirror.

"What am I your guys fucking chauffer?"

"Nah, more like taxi driver." I say with a laugh.

"Yeah, well the meters running bro, I expect some cash when we get home."

"How about I buy you lunch?"

"Really?"

"Yeah."

"Deal. Where you wanna eat?"

"Your choice."

"Alright. I'm cravin' me some Dick's."

"I bet you are." Zoe and I laugh harder then we have probably laughed in months and even Mitch has to laugh at himself.

"That was a good one you little bastard." Zoe and I continue to laugh as we head down the road towards the highway.

We get to Dick's thirty minutes later and enjoy a tasty lunch which consists of burgers, fries, and shakes. After lunch we take Zoe back to her house. I exit the car with her and walk her up to her front door. We stand in front of the door for a few seconds before I finally say something.

"So."

"So." She repeats.

"You want to come over tomorrow night and listen to some records and maybe have some dinner?"

"You gonna make me dinner?" She says with a surprised look on her face.

"Um, make you dinner? No, you wouldn't want me to do that, but I'm a hell of a pizza orderer."

She laughs. "Yeah, that sounds like fun." An awkward silence develops. "I will see you tomorrow then." She says.

"Yeah, see you tomorrow. Around seven?"

"Yeah, seven is fine."

"Okay, see ya then." I think about giving her a hug but I don't and I head back to the car. I turn my head and watch her open the front door and walk inside. I open the front passenger door of the Forester and jump in.

"What was that all about?"

"Nothing. Just invited her over tomorrow night to listen to some records and eat some pizza."

"You asked her out? He says surprised.

"No, I told you we're just friends. It's just two friends enjoying music and pizza. Why is everything about sex and relationships with you?"

"Geez man relax, it just sounds like a date."

At that moment I wonder if Zoe thinks that it's a date. Maybe I should text her and remind her that we are just friends, but I decide not too, for some unknown reason. Mitch puts the Forester in gear and we head off back home.

CHAPTER THIRTEEN

At seven o'clock sharp there is a knock on my door and when I open it, to no surprise it's Zoe. She is holding a large pink and green striped bag like she is ready to hit the beach.

"Hey."

"Hey." I repeat back to her. "Come on in." I move to the side and she walks by me. She is wearing that same perfume and it punches me in the face, but in a good way, if they ever was a good way to get punched in the face. "I was going to order the pizza before you got here but I wasn't sure what you like on it so I thought I would wait."

"Pineapple, jalapenos, mushrooms, and bacon. And not that Canadian bacon garbage, real American bacon."

"You're fucking with me right?"

"What do you mean?"

"Someone told you what I get on my pizza. Who was it? My brother? Dr. Wagner?"

"Nobody told me anything, that's what I always get on my pizzas." I look at her like I don't believe her. "I'm serious Ryan, ask anyone who knows me."

"So it's just an insane coincidence?"

"Yeah, I guess so. It's actually a little freaky now that I think about it."

"Yeah, no shit." I pick up my phone and dial the pizza place. I order an extra-large pineapple, mushroom, jalapeno, and bacon pizza and then hang up. "You want a beer?"

"Sure."

I head to the kitchen and grab two bottles of Sierra Nevada Torpedo out of the refrigerator. I walk back into the living room and hand Zoe one of the bottles.

"Thank you."

"You are welcome."

We head to my bedroom and listen to both sides of *Never Mind the Bollocks Here's the Sex Pistols* while we wait for the pizza to arrive, which it does as the last song, *EMI*, ends, right on cue. I grab the pizza from the delivery guy and give him a twenty. I tell him to keep the change, he thanks me, and I close the door. I take the pizza back to the bedroom and set it down on the bed. I head to the kitchen and grab paper plates, napkins, and a couple more Torpedos. When I get back to the bedroom Zoe is flipping through the records.

"Can we listen to this one?" She holds up The Eagle's *Hotel California*.

"Sure, throw it on. You remember my awesome training from the other night?"

"I hope so." She says with a cute little worried look on her face.

"If not it's cool, it's only a record."

I sit on the bed and put a slice of pizza on each of our plates at the same time watching her as she puts the record on. She does it perfectly and I am thoroughly impressed. She spins around with a huge smile on her face as the title track *Hotel California* begins to play.

"Not bad."

She puts her hands on her hips and gives me a pouty face. "Not bad? I thought I nailed it."

"Whoa, don't get ahead of yourself girl. Come eat."

"Don't tell me what to do." She says in a playful way as she jumps on the bed almost bouncing her pizza right off of it. I shake my head. As the first verse begins I sing along, out loud, but not too loud.

"On a dark desert highway, cool wind in my hair. Warm smell of colitas, rising up through the air. Up ahead in the distance, I saw a shimmering light. My head grew heavy and my sight grew dim. I had to stop for the night."

"You have a good voice, you should sing in a band."

I laugh. "Yeah right." I take a bite of pizza and it's

delicious like it always is.

"Why not?" She takes a bite of hers.

"I have serious stage fright issues. When I was in the seventh grade I was in a school rendition of A Christmas Carol and I forgot my lines and was basically laughed off of the stage by the kids in the audience. I haven't gotten up on a stage since."

She looks at me like I'm crazy. "But you're a teacher?"

"No, I'm a substitute teacher."

"What's the difference?"

"Well, I don't have to know anything. I just do what the real teacher tells me to do. Basically, I'm a babysitter because the kids don't do anything I say anyway, which is fine with me. I don't care what they do as long as no one gets hurt I'm happy."

I hand her a fresh beer, she takes a swig and I do the same. We sit there eating pizza and drinking beer while the Eagles serenade us with *New Kid in Town* and *Life in the Fast Lane*. When the A-side ends we finish up our food and the rest of our current beers. Zoe uses the restroom while I clean up the pizza mess and take it to the kitchen. I set the pizza box on the counter and throw away the plates, napkins, and empty beer bottles. I grab two more Sierra Nevada's from the refrigerator and head back to the bedroom. Zoe exits the bathroom and I hand her a beer.

"Thanks."

"My pleasure." I set my beer on the night stand and head

to use the bathroom.

"Can I put on another record?" Zoe yells through the door.
"Sure."

I finish my business and then start washing my hands when I instantly recognize the song coming through my speakers, its *Calling You* by Blue October, and my first thought is what the fuck? I rinse the soap off of my hands and then dry them off with insane ferocity. I storm through the bathroom door and into the bedroom.

"Are you kidding me right now?" In no way am I joking and she realizes this real quick.

"What?" She says slightly scared.

"Are you kidding me with this song?" I'm getting angrier by the second.

"I don't know what that means Ryan."

I hurry over to the record player, lift the lid, and slap the needle off of the record, which makes a horrible screeching sound. I snatch the record off of the turntable and throw it like a Frisbee. Zoe jumps back as the record comes inches from her head and then smashes into the wall. Black vinyl shrapnel explodes, showering the floor in front of the bed. Zoe looks at me, shocked, as I breathe heavily in and out like I'm some kind of roid raged maniac. I look at her and my anger turns to sadness and then the tears begin to flow. I sit on the ground and cover my face with my hands, still crying. Zoe stands there, frozen, not knowing what to do.

"I'm sorry." I say not even knowing if she is still there.

"It's okay." She says. "I should be the one that's saying sorry."

"Why?" I take my hands off of my face. "How could you have known my issue with that song?" She looks at me like she is about to cry herself.

"I don't know your issue with that song Ryan, but Dr. Wagner must because he told me to find that record and play that song for you."

My jaw drops open. "He told you to do what?" I start to get pissed again.

"He called me and I told him that we had been hanging out and he asked me if I could find the record and then play it for you. I didn't ask why, which I know I should have, but I didn't. I think deep down I didn't want to know. I'm sorry."

"You have nothing to be sorry about, this is on Dr. Wagner." I get angrier as I think more about it. "I can't fucking believe him."

"I'm sure he has his reasons Ryan, he wouldn't do anything to hurt you. He probably just wanted to know how you would react to that song now."

"What do you mean now?"

"Well now that you're seeing me."

"I'm not seeing you, we're just friends." She kneels down next to me.

"And I like being your friend but I want to be more than that." I say nothing. "I'm falling in love with you Ryan." I stare at her. "You're what?"

"I'm falling in love with you." She smiles.

"That's impossible. Why would you want to be with someone who could never love you back?"

Her smile turns upside-down and tears begin to well up in her eyes. "What do you mean?"

"I'm broken Zoe, like that fucking record over there."

"I don't know what that means Ryan." she says as tears slide down her cheeks.

I jump up and run in the direction I tossed the record. I start picking up the pieces like a madman. "I'm broken, like this record." I continue picking up pieces and then I hurry back over to Zoe who is standing up now. "See these pieces?" I hold them out towards her and then toss them on the bed. I start to piece the record back together. "You see I can take all the pieces and try to put them back together." I continue to piece it together. "And I can get some glue and I can try to fix it and even if by some miracle I can get the pieces to stick and hold it won't matter because it won't play, at least not the same as it did before. It's broken, forever, like me. My heart is broken like this vinyl record and it will never be like it was before, it will never love like it did. I can never love you like I love her and I can't do anything about it and you can't do anything about it."

"I can try."

I sit on the bed and shake my head. "It's pointless Zoe. Why would you try? Do you really want to be with someone who loves someone else?"

"Well no."

"See."

"What, do you think I don't have any love in my heart for any of my ex-boyfriends? Cause I do, but those relationships are over and the love I have for you is growing and pushing that other love deep down into my heart where it will stay. Some love never disappears Ryan, we just bury it and focus on the love that is right there in front of our face, the love that has filled our heart to the point that it's about to explode. You will always love her, always, but you have a choice. You can live your life alone or you can bury that love and focus on the love that is right here in front of your face. Look at me" I do what she says. "I'm right here Ryan and I'm not going anywhere. So bury that shit and open your heart to me, you deserve it, we deserve it. We need each other can't you see that?"

I drop my head. "I don't know what I want Zoe. I need some time to think. You should probably go."

She shakes her head. "If that's what you want." She grabs her bag and heads towards the bedroom door but stops before leaving. "Like I said, I'm not going anywhere. You know where I live and where I work so when you figure it out let me know.

"Okay."

She walks back over to me, puts her hand on my shoulder, and kisses the top of my head. "If you need anything just let me know."

"Okay."

She turns and walks out of the room and I hear the front door open and shut seconds later. I sit there like a statue, zoned out, and confused about what just transpired.

Seconds later my brother peeks his head in through the slightly open bedroom door. "You okay?"

I don't look at him. "Not really."

"You wanna talk about it?"

I'm still staring straight ahead. "Not really."

"Okay." He stands there for a few seconds and then goes back to his room. I lie down on the bed and cry myself to sleep.

I stay in bed for the next three days, thinking, contemplating, wondering, fantasizing, dreaming, etc. I get a few calls on my cellphone, but I ignored them and then I just turned it off. I don't eat anything and only drink the water that my brother makes me drink. I haven't showered either and I am beginning to stink up the room. I'm supposed to see Dr. Wagner for my regularly scheduled session in an hour, but I'm still pissed at him so I decide to blow it off. Two hours later there is knock on my bedroom door, but I don't acknowledge it. Then I hear the door open and a familiar voice announce his presence.

"Ryan, can I come in?"

"Go away doc. I'm super pissed at you and I am not sure you want to be in the same room with me right now."

"But I have pizza. Your favorite, pineapple, jalapenos, mushrooms, and bacon."

I could smell it when he opened the door. "Damn it doc." I don't want to see him, but I am starving and that pizza smells amazing. "Alright, bring it over and you better have an explanation for that bullshit you had Zoe do for you."

He walks over and sets the pizza box on the bed. "I'll explain."

"I'm waiting." I say as I lift the pizza box lid and take a slice out.

"I always thought you and Zoe would be good for each other, but I'm not one to play matchmaker in the office. But when Zoe told me that she got a job at a record store the wheels in my head began to turn. I thought that if she could find that record you wanted you would be able to meet her and talk to her outside of the office. That was my only plan, but when she told me you two were hanging out and then when she told me she was falling for you, I decided to see where you were in regards to Shellie. So I asked Zoe if she could find the Blue October record with Calling You on it and then play it for you and then report back to me on how you reacted. It was a little unorthodox, but it was necessary Ryan."

I scarf down a second slice of pizza and stare at him trying to figure out if I still hate him or not.

"I assume she reported back to you?"

He nods his head. "Yes."

"I kinda flipped out a little bit."

"A little bit? You almost killed her with a vinyl record."

I put my right hand on my head realizing now, three days

later, what I had done. And I know it wouldn't have killed her, but the thought of her dead or even injured made my heart hurt. Maybe I was falling for her too. "Shit doc, what did I do? What do I do?"

"You go see her and you apologize, but only if you want to. This has to be your decision, no one else's."

I slide my hand down my face. "Okay doc. I'll go see her, but I can't promise anything. I'm still messed up. I'm still broken."

"I know Ryan, trust me I know. Sometimes it just takes time. She has feeling for you, but she will wait, so just be her friend if that is all you can be right now. Don't run away from her."

"Okay doc. You want some pizza?"

"You know what, I think I will have a slice." Dr. Wagner leans down, grabs a slice, and takes a bite.

"Wow that is good pizza."

"Told you." I get off of the bed and grab the pizza box. "Let's take this to the kitchen. We need napkins and something to drink."

CHAPTER FOURTEEN

After Dr. Wagner leaves I lie in bed and replay everything that has happened over the past couple of week in my head. Listening to records with Zoe. Going on walks with her. Our hike at Twin Falls. And the debacle of the other night. I pass out and wake up a couple of hours later. It is five in the evening and I decide to head to the record store and see if Zoe wants to meet up after she gets off work so we can talk. But before I do I have to shower, I stink. I literally smell like a chimpanzee's sweaty armpit. Not that I know what that smells like, but I'm pretty sure I smell like that if I was to smell a chimp's armpit.

After my shower I get dressed and head to the record store.

It's another chilly evening and I can almost see my breath. I could use a hot beverage and just as that thought crosses my mind I notice that the little coffee shop that Shellie and I use to enjoy is just up ahead. "Fuck it." I say out loud and I head in. I recognize the girl behind the counter and she smiles and seems to recognize me.

"Hey, how have you been? I haven't seen you in here in a while."

"Yeah it's been a few months." I think to myself please God don't let her mention Shellie.

"So where's the girl you always come in with?" Thanks a lot God, geez.

"Um, we're not together anymore." I say with more ease than I would have thought.

"Oh, I'm sorry to hear that."

"Yeah, well that's how life goes sometimes…So can I get two large lattes to go please?"

"Sure thing."

She goes and makes the coffees and I take a seat in the nearest chair. After a couple minutes she returns with the two coffees. I pay her, thank her, and then leave. I get to the record store and realize that I can't open the door because I have to pull it to open it and my hands are full. So I knock, but the music is too loud inside and no one hears me. I look through the glass door and try to get someone's attention but it is mostly covered with advertisements for new records and band gig flyers.

"Need some help?" I recognize the voice immediately and I turn around.

"I thought you were working already?"

"Nope, they cut my hours, I'm only working from six to ten now." I notice she is wearing my U-dub hoodie and it looks way better on her than on me. "What do ya got there?" She looks at the coffees I am holding and so do I.

"Um, I brought you a coffee." I look back at her and extend my right hand. She takes it and smiles.

"Thank you."

"No problem. Look I came here not just to give you a coffee but also to see if you wanted to talk later. Maybe when you get off work?"

"Yeah, I would love to chat. How about my place? Say...ten-thirty?"

"Yeah, okay, great, I'll see you then."

"Okay."

We walk past each other and I stop and turn around. "Zoe." She turns around. "Yeah."

"I'm gonna say it again later tonight, but I want you to know that I'm really sorry about the other night. I just..."

She interrupts me. "It's okay Ryan. I forgave you the second it happened." She smiles and enters the record store.

I stand there for several seconds mesmerized by how fucking cool she is and then I turn and walk back home. On the way home I decide to head to another record store and pick up a little I'm sorry gift for Zoe. I'm not sure if she even has a record player, but I figure if I get her a record she will have to get one and it's a win-win for everyone. When I get home I decide to wrap it, but the only wrapping paper says Happy Birthday all over it in large multi-colored letters. Oh well, no one ever looks at the wrapping paper anyway.

At ten my brother comes into my room. "Let's go."

I look at him. "It's only ten. It doesn't take thirty minutes to get there."

"Yeah I know but I want to stop somewhere on the way. Now put your pants on and let's go."

"Alright. I put my pants on and then my shoes and we walk to the car.

"What's that?" He points to the wrapped record I'm holding.

"Just a little I'm sorry gift for Zoe."

"Oh, it's not her birthday?" Of course my brother would notice the wrapping paper.

"It's the only wrapping paper we had." He shakes his head. "So where are we going?"

"The supermarket."

"What for?"

"Flowers."

I'm confused. "Flowers? You have a hot date tonight?"

"No, they're for you."

"Oh thanks bro that's sweet but I don't own a vase."

"They're not actually for you, they're for you to give to Zoe."

"Why would I give her flowers?"

"Because that's what guys do. Don't get me wrong a record is cool, but flowers are better, trust me."

"I don't know that might give her the wrong impression."

"Oh yeah, you're just friends."

"Exactly."

"Then give her some yellow roses, I'm pretty sure yellow signifies friendship."

"Yeah but roses don't."

"Then get her some lilies or tulips or daisies or whatever, it doesn't matter, it's the thought that counts."

"Alright, I guess I could give her some flowers. Friends do that right?"

"Of course they do." The smirk on my brother's face reminds me of when used to mess with me when we were kids and I glare back at him.

"You messin' with me?"

He starts laughing. "No man, just relax." I don't believe him.

After we pick up the flowers, a dozen multi-colored tulips, which I perceive as the friendliest arrangement they had, we head to Zoe's place. We get there at ten-thirty on the dot. I hop out with the flowers and turn around as Mitch hands me the record.

"Good luck Ryno. Call me if you need a ride home."

"Thanks, but I'll probably just walk."

"You'll freeze to death, just call me, I don't care what time it is."

"Alright, alright, see ya later." I turn and make my way up the walkway, holding the bouquet of flowers and the record. I notice the lights are on, which I assume means she's home. I hear Mitch drive off as I hit the doorbell. A few seconds later Zoe answers the door. Her pink hair is pulled back into a loose ponytail and she is smiling.

"Hey there." She is wearing a cute little Houndstooth dress and she's barefoot. I am mesmerized by the pattern on her dress and it takes a few seconds for me to respond.

"Hey."

She notices the flowers immediately. "And what are those?"

I look at the flowers. "It was my brother's idea." I blurt out. I hand her the flowers and she takes them.

"Well, tell your brother thank you and that I love them."

"Okay." I say, which makes her laugh.

"I was kidding Ryan, geez, you're such a gull-i-bull." She notices the wrapped record in my other hand. "And what is that?" She points to it. "Are you going to a birthday party after this?" Unbelievable, apparently everyone looks at the damn wrapping paper.

"No, it's my I'm sorry gift, it was the only wrapping paper we had, I didn't think you would notice."

She laughs. "Ryan, it says Happy Birthday in huge multi-colored letters how could I not notice it?"

I look at it. "True."

"Come on in and have a seat on the couch while I put these in some water.

"Okay." I take a seat on the couch, holding the wrapped record and I notice it immediately.

"You have a record player." I yell from the living room.

"I do. I had to, I mean I do work at a record store and my...well you have one so..." She yells from the kitchen. She comes back into the living room holding a vase filled with water and the tulips. "What do you think?"

I look at her, not the flowers. "Beautiful."

She smiles as she walks over and sets the vase on the coffee table. "You want to listen to a record?"

"Yeah, of course. Maybe we can listen to this one." I hold out the gift and she takes it.

"Thanks for ruining the surprise."

"Shit, sorry."

"I knew it was a record silly." She starts laughing.

"What's so funny?"

"I just realized the irony."

"The irony?"

"Yeah, you almost killed me with a record and to say sorry you're giving me a record. Oh my God, if this is that record..."

I cut her off. "It's not that record that record can burn in hell." She smiles and begins to remove the wrapping paper, delicately like she plans on keeping it for use later. When she is finally done she stares at it. "Have you heard of him?"

"I haven't." She flips the cover to the back.

"He's great, one of my favorites." The record is *Time Without Consequences* by Alexi Murdoch. "You want to listen to it."

"I would love to. You want to put it on while I go grab us a couple of beers?"

"Sure." I stand up and grab the record from her. I unwrap it as I walk over to the record player. I lift up the tinted plastic lid, take the record out of its sleeve, and place it on the turntable. I turn it on, take the needle off of its rest and gently set it down at the beginning of track six, a song called *Wait*.

Zoe returns from the kitchen with two beers and she hands me one as we sit down on the couch, an entire cushion is between us. As the song goes into its first verse I can see that she is listening to the lyrics, which I was hoping she would do. We look at each other and smile. When the chorus begins I quietly lip the words as I look at her.

"And if I stumble, and if I stall, and if I slip now, and if I should fall, and if I can't be all that I could be, will you...will you wait for me. " She smiles and gives me a little nod acknowledging that she gets what I am trying to say without actually saying it. I have a tendency to speak through songs and records, I always have. I'm not sure if it's the coward in me or the romantic in me, I guess that's up to whoever is listening to decide.

When the song ends she gets up and turns the volume down, but not off and then sits back down on the couch in the same spot.

"I have some things to say."

I have no idea what is coming. "Okay."

"First, know that I understand what you're going through, love is a motherfucker, we can all attest to that. Secondly, if you just want to be friends I am totally cool with that. And lastly, I'm ready to talk about my family if you want to know what happened to them?"

"Okay." I don't know if I'm ready now that she's ready, but here we go.

"And just so you know, there's no need to say you're sorry about what happened to them or anything like that, just listen, okay?"

"Okay."

"Ten months ago my dad and little brother were driving back from Portland after a Trailblazers game. My brother was a huge basketball fan and as you probably know the Sonics are now in Oklahoma City and the closest team is in Portland. Anyway, it had been raining all day in most of western Washington and the roads were slick. Just south of Olympia a car merged onto I-5 and almost hit a car, which made that car swerve and when it did it hit my dad's car. My dad lost control of the car and it flipped several times and that was that."

Tears begin to slide down her cheeks and I am not far behind. She wipes them away with her right hand and continues. "My mom got the call and all I saw was her fall to the ground, the phone bouncing off of the carpet. We didn't even need to go to the hospital. They died right there on that fucking highway."

She takes a deep breath and I just look at her and continue to listen like she said. "We buried them four days later. My dad was forty-eight." She pauses as more tears slid down her cheeks. "My brother was twelve. He had his entire life ahead of him and that was snuffed out just like that, in one split second." She wipes the tears from her cheeks. "Anyway, neither one of us handled it very well. I started cutting myself which led to my mother putting me on anti-depressants because she didn't want me to kill myself, which is ironic because she refused to take them and then she was the one that killed herself."

I shake my head in disbelief and tears begin to slide down my cheeks. The shit that she has gone through makes my little heartbreak pity party seem like nothing. And at that moment I fall in love with her, but say nothing as I continue to listen like she told me to. "So then I had to bury my mother two months after burying my father and brother. That led to me cutting again and almost killing myself, which led to me having to see Dr. Wagner, and here we are eight months later and I'm still trying to find the purpose in all of this." I stare at her. "Why are you staring at me like that?"

"You told me not to say or do anything so I don't know what to do."

She cracks a tiny smile. "I did, didn't I? Well you're a very good listener and I'm glad that I finally told someone what happened besides Dr. Wagner.

"Well, I feel honored that you told me and I am sorry about your loss." She glares at me. "Sorry, I had to, its human nature." She wipes the tears from her face.

"Okay, enough with all the sorry's and this depressing shit let's listen to some music and drink some beers.

"Sounds good to me."

Zoe heads to the kitchen to grab more beers and I head to the record player to put on a new record. "Put on something a little more upbeat." She yells from the kitchen.

"Okay." I yell back. I take a few seconds to flip through her record collection, which isn't really a collection. It's a dozen records in a light blue milk crate.

"Holy shit, you have *Beelzebubba* by the Dead Milkmen? I used to have this on cassette tape when I was like ten years old, I love this record." I yell. She walks back into the living room holding two beers.

"Yeah I came across it a couple days ago at the store and it looked interesting especially the song titles. I haven't listened to it yet though."

"ex-squeeze me? Baking powder? You haven't listened to this yet?"

"Nope."

"Well hell, I guess there is no better time than now." I put the Alexi Murdoch record back in its cover and then put The Dead Milkmen record on the turntable and gently drop the needle on track one, *Brat in the Frat*. "Now you are either going to love this or hate it, there is no in-between when it comes to the Milkmen.

Surprisingly she loves it, which is weird because ninety-five percent of people hate it. We spend the next thirty minutes dancing in the living room and drinking beers. I can't believe she's fallen for me and that I'm falling for her. I have no idea what will happen, but I know that right now it is perfect and it's what we both need in our broken lives.

When the record ends we fall back onto the couch, exhausted and slightly intoxicated.

"So Ryan, are you a dog person or a cat person?" Her question comes out of nowhere and it honestly throws me off a bit.

"Um, neither I guess. I mean I don't have any pets so…"

"But if you did what would you get a dog or a cat?

"Zoe, I can barely take care of myself let alone an animal."

"I'm not telling you to get a pet Ryan, it's a hypothetical question. Okay let's say I wanted to get a pet, what would you suggest I get?"

"Wow, that's a serious question."

"What do you mean?"

"I mean you're basically asking me to tell you who you are as a person. And even if I told you what to get you would still get what you wanted."

She looks at me like I'm nuts. "Dog or cat Ryan? Just say dog or cat for Christ's sake."

"Dog or Cat" I smile, she doesn't and just glares at me.

"Okay, cat."

"Really? I thought you would be a dog person."

"See, you don't even know who I am, I'm outta here." I act like I'm going to get up and leave and then just sit back down and we laugh.

"So why a cat?" she asks.

"Well, mainly because they can take care of themselves. You don't have to take them outside to shit or piss. With a cat you basically just have to feed them and clean their litter box. Oh and cats don't bark, I fucking hate barking dogs, even more than honking car horns. So why all the dog and cat questions?"

"Oh I was just curious. I was thinking about getting a dog, but I'm not sure."

"Oh yeah, what kind?"

"A Chihuahua." She smiles unusually big and I'm not sure why. "Do you like Chihuahuas?" She is still grinning from ear to ear. And then it hits me, she knows about the dog kicking incident.

I decide to play dumb. "Yeah, I love small dogs like that?"

She looks surprised by my answer. "Really?"

"Yeah they're great." Now I'm smiling and her smile turns to a frown. We stare at each other of a good twenty seconds.

"Oh come on Ryan, tell me about the dog kicking incident."

"How the hell do you know about...ooooh, Dr. Wagner, that bastard. Isn't that a breach of confidentiality or something?"

"Oh stop it, who cares, just tell me what happened it has been killing me for weeks now."

"I thought he told you?"

"No he just mentioned an incident between you and a Chihuahua and that was it, he totally left me hangin'."

"Oh, well it's not much of a story. I was on a walk, this Chihuahua jumped off its porch and came at me barking so I kicked it." Her mouth is wide open. "It was reactionary. I had nothing against that dog, it just barked up the wrong tree."

Zoe starts laughing uncontrollably and then finds her bearings several seconds later. "And that was it?"

"Well then the dog's owner came running from the porch. She picked up the dog and started cursing me out big-time, I think she even called me a motherfucker."

Zoe starts laughing again. "Well now it all makes sense."

"Is there anything else he told you that I need to explain?" I was joking.

"Well..." My eyes get wide.

"Are you serious?"

"There was just one more thing."

"What was it?"

"Something about a squirrel." She smiles.

I roll my eyes and then start laughing. "That was nothing."

"Tell me, tell me, tell me." She's like a five year old girl wanting to hear a joke that her father can't tell her because it's inappropriate.

"Okay, geez. There was this squirrel that hung out in the tree in our front yard and he would come down and look and me and I would talk to him." I shrug my shoulders. "Dr. Wagner was worried but I told him I was just saying things like hey what's up when he came down and see ya later when he ran off. It wasn't like the squirrel was talking back. If it did talk back I would be in the looney bin right now."

She looks disappointed in my explanation. "Well that wasn't what I had though had happened."

"What did you think happened?"

"Well my best guess was that a squirrel took your keys and ran up a tree and you climbed the tree and then fell out of the tree almost killing yourself."

I start laughing. "Yeah, that's a much better story."

After her investigative questioning about my craziness we lie on the floor and watch *Away We Go* on Netflix, which is a cute little movie featuring songs by Alexi Murdoch, including *Wait*, the song I played for her earlier. We pass out in each other's arms and wake up the next morning with the TV still on. We get up and walk to a nearby diner and share a huge stack of buttermilk pancakes. When we finish we say goodbye outside the diner, hug, and go our separate ways.

CHAPTER FIFETEEN

    I spend the day thinking about Zoe and what has occurred over the past twenty-four hours. What she said last night and the other night replay in my head over and over. I feel like an idiot, but I also feel like I am not alone and that gives me comfort. What she has gone through over the past ten months is unreal and it puts my life in perspective. My loss was brutal, but hers was unimaginable and it changes my whole idea of what pain is. I call her after she gets off work.

    "Hey."

    "Hey. How are you?" she asks.

    "I'm good. How are you doing?"

    "I'm doing good also."

"I'm happy to hear that. So I was thinking that maybe we could meet up at Harbor Park tomorrow.

"Yeah, that sounds good."

"Do you know where it is?"

"Yeah, I've been there before."

"Okay, cool. I was thinking noon."

"That works for me."

"Great. I'll see you then."

"Okay. See ya tomorrow Ryan."

I hit the end call button on my cellphone and toss it on my night stand.

The next morning I wake up to the alarm on my cellphone. It's ten and I don't waste any time getting ready for my meet up with Zoe. I shower, get dressed, and then head to the kitchen to make a pot of coffee. Mitch is nowhere to be seen so I decide to take the bus to Harbor Park.

After three cups of coffee I head to the bus stop. I jump on the bus, which is practically empty except for an older lady and a couple of teenagers who I assume are a couple and are skipping school. They are holding hands and I imagine Zoe and I doing the same on the beach in the near future.

I get to the park fifteen minutes early and I decide to wait in the branchless tree forest, which is basically about fifty skinny trees with no branches right there in the sandy beach. This place is awesome. I look for Zoe the entire fifteen minutes and then I see her walking, looking around for me. I walk over to her and she sees me before I reach her.

"Hey there." She says with a smile.

"Hey." I smile back. "You wanna go sit on the beach and talk."

"Sure." We walk side by side towards the sand and the water that is Puget Sound. Our hands brush against each other's as we walk and this time I get the courage to hold her hand. She looks at me and smiles. We reach a nice place about twenty yards from the water and sit down on the cold sand. "So Ryan is this just a hang out or do you have something you want to say to me."

"Both I guess." She looks at me, waiting for me to continue. "I just wanted to say that I really appreciate you telling me what you told me the other night, but what I really want to do is to explain to you what I've been going through. I mean you opened up to me and it's only fair that I do the same."

"Okay."

"Well, four months ago, on our second anniversary, my girlfriend left me for another guy. She was the love of my life and it crushed me. I was going to propose to her that night, but never got a chance to. I started cutting myself and avoiding everyone. I was having serious thoughts of suicide one night so I called the suicide hotline and they told me to go into my local psych clinic, which I did. They talked with me and then gave me a prescription for some anti-depressants. Then I moved in with my brother and basically spent two months in bed. Then I started seeing Dr. Wagner and then I met you and now here I am." She smiles and puts her hand on my knee. "I know my loss is nothing like yours, but it still fucked me up. I'm broken Zoe and I don't know if I can ever be fixed."

"Loss is loss Ryan. Losing a parent or a sibling or a girlfriend or a wife or whatever is hard, losing anything is hard. People deal with it in different ways. Some people just cry, some people cut, some people end up not being able to handle it, like my mother, and they kill themselves. You handled your loss how you did because that was how you were supposed to handle it, just like me. We've survived our loss, that's what's important. We are alive and we can enjoy this beach and we can enjoy delicious food and can enjoy vinyl records and we can enjoy each other's company and so on. The past is the past and it's time for both of us to put it behind us and move on."

She is right but I don't tell her that. "Maybe it is." I say instead.

As we sit there we watch other couples walk along the beach and we have some fun by making up ridiculous conversations that they might be having. We watch people feeding the seagulls and fishermen casting into the bitter cold water from the beach. Clouds roll in after about an hour and the temperature dips a bit so we cuddle up to keep warm. It is a perfect afternoon. We lie there for a couple hours, relaxing, and just enjoying each other's company. Around three we have to go because Zoe has work. We jump on the bus and head towards our neighborhoods.

"So can I come over tonight after work?" she asks me.

"Yeah, of course."

"Sweet."

My stop comes quicker that I had wanted it to, but that's how it goes sometimes. I give Zoe a hug and tell her that I will see her later. She kisses me on the cheek and I hop off the bus. I turn around and we lock eyes as the bus takes off down the street. I turn and head home with a huge smile on my face.

At ten-thirty sharp there is a soft knock on the front door. I barely hear it, but I was expecting it, and I jump up to answer it. It's Zoe and she is wearing my U-Dub hoodie, her pink hair matching well with the purple pullover. She is holding her big pink and green striped beach bag.

"Hey."

"Hey, come on in." I say as I move to the side. She walks by me and her perfume punches me in the face again. I shut the door and follow her to my room. When we get there I sit on the bed and she just stands there staring at me. "What are you staring at?" I say playfully.

She reaches into her big beach bag, pulls something out of it, and extends it towards me. "What's that?" I look at it and it looks awfully familiar. Happy Birthday is written all over it in large multi-colored letters and I realize that it's the same wrapping paper I used to wrap the record I got her. No wonder she was so careful with it.

"It's just a little something I thought you would enjoy." She takes a step towards me and I take it from her. I can tell by the shape and feel that it is indeed a vinyl record.

"You do remember what happened the last time you brought me a record don't you?"

"Yes Ryan I remember, just take it out and look at it."

I tear the wrapping paper off like a kid on Christmas morning and to no surprise it's a vinyl record, *X & Y* by Coldplay to be exact. I stare at it not knowing what to think.

"You like it?" she asks and I look up at her. She is smiling.

"I do. Thank you." I look back at the record.

"Can I play it for you?" I look back at her.

"Of course."

She takes it from me and takes off the plastic that was protecting it. She walks over to the record player and lifts the lid. I sit down on the bed and watch her. She takes the record carefully out of its jacket and places it even more carefully on the turntable. She switches it on, lifts the needle from its rest, and places it on the record. I notice the song right away, it's *Fix You*, and my heart begins to race. Then I realize why she bought me that record and why she's playing this particular song and my eyes begin to well up with tears. She turns around and smiles at me and I smile back as the tears begin to slide down my cheeks. She walks up to me, still smiling, and kneels down in front of me. She takes my hands and looks straight into my eyes. I look back at hers and my heart jumps out of my chest.

"I don't care how broken you are, have been, or will be. I love you Ryan, and I will be here, by your side, through all of it. And I promise that no matter what happens, I will try to fix you." I smile, tears still sliding, and I pull her up. I embrace her and then whisper in her ear.

"You already have Zoe. You already have." We embrace tighter. "I guess you found your purpose huh?"

She starts crying and I can feel her warm tears on my neck. I loosen my hold on her and kiss her forehead. She looks at me and I kiss her cheek. I can taste her salty tears as I make my way to her lips. And I finally kiss her with all the passion in my soul and it's electric. It's like we are up in space, just the two of us, floating up there, holding each other, kissing. We are two celestial beings in one perfect cosmic moment. And then I wake up and realize that it was all just a dream…I'm just kidding, but honestly, it did feel like a dream and even though we are not perfect, we are perfect for each other and we are alive and that is all that really matters…isn't it?

Love is still a motherfucker.

I love you and miss you dad.

(T.A. Maxwell Sr. 1954-2012)

The Following Pages Contain a Sneak Peak

of T.A. Maxwell's Novel:

Into the Ocean

"Damn it's hot out here." I say out loud, to myself, as I stand on one of the many banks of the mighty Colorado River just outside Yuma, Arizona. I think I'm still in California though, but maybe not. I'm not completely sure. Well, I'm pretty sure. I'm on the western side of the River and I think that's still California. It doesn't really matter I guess. I'm holding a heavy duty tan cardboard container about the size of a shoebox if it was taller and not as long. Inside said box is my grandfather, or at least what is left of him. As the sun beats down on my white skin adding color to it, which will more than likely be red since I forgot to put sunscreen on, I look up at the sun. I close my eyes just about as soon as my eyes meet it and I can still see its shape behind my eyelids. Beads of sweat roll down my forehead and down my cheeks. I can feel sweat from my neck meandering its way down my chest towards my stomach and down my back towards my you know what. The sun is blazing hot. It feels like when you reach in to grab a casserole out of the oven. That dry, baking heat that makes you wonder why anyone would live in such a place. Yuma is one of the hottest places in the United States, basically hell on earth.

I lower my head, open my eyes, and stare at the Colorado River. For some unknown reason I suddenly imagine in my mind a single flake of snow falling from the sky and gently resting on the side of a Colorado mountain peak a thousand miles away. I watch it slowly melt under the early summer sun and combine with a million other melted snowflakes, gravity forcing the cool water down the mountainside to form a tiny stream below. Then they meet up with a billion other melted snowflakes from other tiny streams and become the mighty Colorado River. They rush west through southern Utah and then carve through the Grand Canyon. Then they take a sharp left separating California and Arizona, before they flow into Mexico, eventually emptying into and become part of the Sea of Cortez, which becomes a part of the Pacific Ocean, the largest body of water on Earth.

As I watch the flowing water, I am witnessing that incredible journey, the journey of a billion tiny snowflakes over and over again. The heat is gone, but only in my mind. A honey bee buzzes by my left ear, violently breaking my trance. I shake my head and swat at my ear with my left hand hoping to avoid a sting. I check the ground to see if I got lucky and knocked that little bastard out, but I see nothing, only dirt and dried up bushes.

I look back at the river and then beyond it, which I believe is the Arizona side, but I am not a hundred percent sure. On the other bank, the eastern bank, there are a couple of beat to hell mobile homes. The sea green siding of one of them is half gone and the weeds are so out of control I can't even see the bottom half of the thing. The other one is in worse shape, with cardboard acting as a window and tin foil acting as another one. The weeds are more under control in front of this one, enough that I can make out a small kiddie pole in the yard. It's one of those hard blue plastic pools with cartoon looking fish on it that you see in front of every Wal-Mart during the summer months. I look back at the Colorado and take a deep breath as the desert oven kicks it up a notch to the completely unbearable setting.

Of course he wanted his ashes dumped into this particular river and of course he had to leave this earth in the middle of July. And of course, I, Camp Kershaw, the oldest and only living descendant had to fulfill his final wishes. But I was actually okay with it. My grandfather was a great man, an honest man, a man who was well respected around town and worked hard all the way up until his final breath. He was a businessman, owned three small hardware stores in the greater San Diego area. His heart gave out in aisle five, of the first and largest store, next to the sandpaper. He was helping a young woman choose the correct grit so she could refinish an old table that she was going to give as a gift to her soon-to-be mother-in-law. When he fell, she screamed, and Johnny, a part-time summer employee who was about to enter his senior year of high school, came running. Johnny didn't really know what to do so he called 911 and an ambulance arrived seven minutes later. My grandfather never made it to the hospital. He died right there in aisle five doing what he loved. I was told later that day that he died from Sudden Cardiac Death, which basically means his heart just stopped or something. He had a heart attack a couple of years ago, which didn't seem to faze him, but this one stopped him dead in his tracks, so to speak.

A cool breeze hit me making the sweat all over my body feels like little drops of cold rain, but only for a second. The blazing hot desert sun brought me back to reality real quick. I look at the cardboard urn and decide that it's probably time to dump these ashes, sorry, my grandfather, and hop back into the car where there's air conditioning. The thought makes me smile, but then I realize what I am about to do and the smile disappears. I open the temporary urn and stare at the ashes, which are in a plastic bag. I remove the twist tie and shove it into my front left pants pocket. I open the plastic bag and look at the grey dust, small bits of bone still present throughout. I guess I should probably say something.

"Grandfather…" I say a bit too loud so I tone it down, I am the only one here. "…you taught me many things during your life. You taught me the importance of an education." I think of what to say next. "You taught me table manners and other types of…etiquette stuff." I had nothing written down of course, I was totally winging it. "You were kind to me and when mom and dad died you took me in and raised me the best you could, even though I was fifteen and already set in most of my ways." I pause again and try to think of something else to say. "I remember the day I came to live with you. It was the day after mom and dad were put in the ground. I was staying with Aunt Carol at the house, but she had to head back to Denver that morning. You answered your door, gave me a half smile, and then gave me a side hug. I knew right then and there that I would be okay and that you would help ease the pain of our loss." Tears join the beads of sweat that are sliding down my cheeks. "I will never forget you and I will live the rest of my life honoring you by trying to be as great a man as you were."

With that, I kneel down and empty the contents of the tan cardboard urn into the somewhat warm waters of the mighty Colorado River. My grandfather's ashes hitch a ride on the current, but dissolve and disappear soon after they enter the moving water. He has become one with the river. Small amounts of his ashes never reach the water and are kidnapped and taken away by the wind. When the urn is finally empty I place the top back on it and stand up. I stand there for several seconds thinking about my grandfather, well actually just picturing his face. I look back up at the sun and I quickly look away as its blinding light and heat burns my retinas. I look back at the mighty Colorado and sigh, shoulders rise and fall. I turn and proceed to walk, slowly, towards my car, which is really my grandfather's car, but if you want to get technical I guess it is mine now. I quickly realize that the A/C is waiting for me so I pick up the pace. When I get back to the car I toss the empty cardboard urn in the trunk. Then I get in the driver's seat, turn on the ignition, crank up the A/C, put the car in gear, and head back towards San Diego on Interstate 8.

The drive west through the southern part of California is incredibly boring. The scenery is bland and there is not much to look at. And since I can't pass the time looking at anything interesting I decide to pass the time thinking about my grandfather. The first thing that pops in my head is why the hell he wanted his remains to be poured into the Colorado River. I mean why not the Pacific Ocean? He was born in San Diego, he lived in San Diego, and he died in San Diego. And the last time I checked the great city of San Diego bordered the largest ocean on the planet. I don't remember him ever talking about the Colorado River and I can't remember seeing any pictures of him in or on or around it. Maybe he always wanted to but never got the chance. Maybe one of his dreams was to float down the mighty Colorado. If it was one of his dreams he sure as hell didn't tell me about it.

The sun is finally beginning to fall towards the western horizon. It is four o'clock and home, San Diego, is still a few hours away. I scan the inside of his car, which is probably my car now, but that is not official yet. It is a 2009 Audi A6 sedan, a nice car, but way too much for me. I am not a businessman or a lawyer or a doctor and I have no need for a car like this. My plan, if it's left to me, which I'm pretty sure it is, is to sell it as soon as it is official and buy something more my style, which just means cheaper, and then after that, I have no idea. I have only been home for a couple of months after spending a year in China teaching English at various secondary schools in and around Beijing. I had planned on going back for one more year but now I don't really feel up to it. Besides, I was getting irritated teaching English to a bunch of commie Chinese kids who were only learning the language so they could attend American colleges so one day they could take us over and the world. Or maybe I'm just being paranoid, or maybe not, I don't know, I hate politics.

My thoughts on China leave my head as quickly as they appeared and I once again envision my grandfather's face. He was eighty years old when he died in aisle five of Kershaw's flagship hardware store. He was single, married twice, but only had one child, a son, my father. His first wife, Margie divorced him after she found out he was doing more than just helping out a woman who needed a part-time job, if you know what I mean. His second wife, Vivian had a stroke and died in the bathtub as she was getting ready for their thirtieth wedding anniversary dinner. My parents died three months later in a car accident. 1995 was a terrible year for the entire family.

Like I said earlier, my grandfather took me in after the death of my parents, I was fifteen and about to start my sophomore year of high school. That entire school year was tough for both of us. My grades slipped from A's and B's to C's and D's as my grandfather battled depression and a slight addiction to pain killers. The summer before my junior year I snapped out of it after a near fatal cliff diving incident in Cabo San Lucas. A near death experience makes you wake up real quick. My grandfather, around the same time, kicked the pain med addiction after a short stint at a posh rehabilitation center in Oceanside, just up the Interstate.

During the next two years I got my grades back up and

graduated with a 2.99 grade point average, a hundredth of a point from a 3.0, just my luck. It didn't matter anyway, it wasn't like I was headed to Stanford or USC or anything. I did end up trying college, well community college, and it wasn't really for me, at least not at the time. I was nineteen and had no idea what I wanted to do with my life so I went to work full-time with the guy I worked with part-time during high school. His name was Steve and he was basically a handyman, a do-a-little-bit-of-everything-guy. He worked for my grandfather at store number two when he was in his twenties. Then he went to work for himself because he hated someone telling him what hours to work and when, at least that's what he told me. He was an independent, free spirit kind of guy, not a hippie, just a cool, laidback dude.

I met Steve when I was sixteen after my grandfather told me it was time for me to get a job. There would be no discussion; it was a requirement, to teach me the value and reward of hard work he would say. He, of course, said I could work at one of the hardware stores, but then suggested I go work with Steve. I think he wanted me to have a father figure that was closer to the age of an actual father. Anyway, Steve took me under his wing with no hesitation and taught me everything he knew. By the time I graduated high school I could install toilets and air conditioner ducts, change the oil in anything, paint an entire house inside and out, repair any small engine, and complete a plethora of other tasks and odd jobs. When it came time for college, both Steve and my grandfather pushed me to at least give it a shot, which I did.

When college didn't work out I went back to work with

Steve like I said. Two years later I tried college again and this time stuck with it. I continued to work with Steve when I could and five years later I graduated with a bachelor's degree in construction management from San Diego State University. Both of the men in my life were proud of my accomplishment, but it would have never happened without their push and support and of course their money. After college I went back to work with Steve full-time and we had a pretty good thing going. I really had no plans to leave and "use the degree" I had just spent five years completing.

A few years later Steve officially made me his partner. I was twenty nine years old and doing pretty well for myself. Then two days before my thirty-second birthday Steve was rear ended while he was stopped at a red light, which wouldn't have been that big of deal if he was in his truck, but he wasn't. He was on his Indian, his baby, the motorcycle he had just finished restoring. He died at the scene and I had lost the third important person in my life, because someone thought that it was more important to respond to a text message than to focus on the road. This was three years ago.

The first year after Steve's death I did nothing. I couldn't work and I barely ate, which caused me to lose twenty pounds, weight that I didn't have to lose. Steve had put me down as his only beneficiary on his life insurance policy, which I was unaware of until I received a phone call telling me so. Most of the two hundred and fifty thousand dollars was gone quickly after taxes, paying off the rest of my student loans, and my decision to donate some of it to various charities that Steve had supported over the years. I have never really been a guy that got all excited over money. The way I look at it, as long as I have a roof over my head, clothes on my back, and food in my belly, I'm good. With the rest of the life insurance money I travelled the country in Steve's yellow 1985 Volkswagen Westfalia van, which he left me in his will, which was really just a handwritten piece of paper I found in his sock drawer. He left his truck to another friend of his and of course his share of the business went to me.

As I continue west on Interstate 8 through the southern-most part of California I notice the U.S./Mexico border just outside my driver's side window. The fence doesn't look that high and I immediately imagine a couple of Mexicans attempting to pole vault over it. Not sure why that popped in my head, but I think there was a news story about such an incident not too long ago. I fixate my eyes back on the road in front of me just as a semi passes by at seventy miles an hour, which makes me jump and my heart beat a tad faster. The sun is slowly making its way down like a slow motion replay of a jump shot during an NBA basketball game. I turn on the radio and *The Stroke* by Billy Squire is playing. I smile and think about Steve again, he loved this song and so do I.

On the one year anniversary of Steve's death I headed back to San Diego after almost nine months on the road. During that time I visited every state in the union, except Alaska and Hawaii. I saw the Grand Canyon in Arizona, Carlsbad Caverns in New Mexico, the French Quarter in New Orleans, and the sun rise and set in the Florida Keys. I toured Philadelphia, New York City, and Boston and climb to the top of the highest peak in Maine, Mt. Katahdin. I also drove through the rust belt, the Bible belt, the Great Plains, the Pacific Northwest, and finally the Great Basin. I met tons of people, picked up several hitchhikers, and learned a lot about myself. It took a month or so for me to snap out of it and get back to work. The insurance money drying up had also pushed me a little bit and I had driven the Westfalia to death, literally. Our business wasn't dead though, but it was definitely on life support. I had two employees who had kept it afloat while I was off "finding myself."

A car passes me at a high rate of speed ending the memory. I curse the driver under my breath as I continue on towards San Diego, which is not too far away. The sun has now disappeared and darkness begins to cover everything like cold dirt covering a casket that was just set down into a six foot hole. As I reach the city limits of my hometown I think about Steve and my grandfather and wonder when it will be my turn to dissolve into some body of water. Will it be a river like my grandfather or a lake like Steve? Or maybe I'll just become part of the great Pacific Ocean? I should probably decide soon because who knows what will happen in the near future. Death can happen at any moment. That is how delicate life is. Just like that, we are dust.

www.ingramcontent.com/pod-product-compliance
Lightning Source LLC
Chambersburg PA
CBHW031318120626
46554CB00001BA/452

* 9 7 8 0 9 8 9 0 1 8 2 6 5 *